About the Author

Frank Dirscherl is the author of many novels, including the Amazon bestselling *The Wraith* and *Sanderson of Metro,* as well as several short stories. His *The Wraith Dread Avenger of the Underworld* books have been enjoyed by readers all over the world.

A librarian with over thirty years experience, Frank has also worked at a book wholesaler, a specialist medical practice and as a tutor in the writing and producing of comic books. His interests include reading, traveling, politics, architecture and the environment.

Frank lives in the Illawarra on the south coast of New South Wales, Australia, with his wife and daughter, and is always working on his latest literary endeavors.

Praise for *Sanderson of Metro*
Amazon bestseller

"Once shrouded in mystery, The Wraith's stunning origin is finally revealed. Dirscherl and Nash have written one hell of an adventure novel filled with myth, intrigue, and excitement. Highly recommended reading."
  - A.P. Fuchs, writer, *The Axiom-man Saga, The Way of the Fog, Undead World trilogy*

"Recommended for Wraith and pulp hero fans."
  - Leon Mallett, *Amazon*

"At the end of the day, this novel is a worthy addition to The Wraith's continuing story and a necessary purchase if you're a fan of the character. It's also just a flat out enjoyable reading experience."
  - Marcus Bucklin, *Amazon*

"The story is well written, and the Paul Sanderson character fleshed out fairly well...I highly recommend this well written entry for all comic book fans."
  - Virginia E. Johnson, *Amazon*

Praise for *The Wraith*
Amazon bestseller

"I love the coloring job and specially the 'glowing' eyes on the chest of the character."
   – Guillermo del Toro, director, *Blade II, Hellboy I & II*

"I liked the story a lot... It's a very strong debut."
   Steve Englehart, writer, *Detective Comics, The Avengers, Green Lantern*

"I have read the novel (I couldn't put it down)... It is amazing to see how her (Leena) character evolves from Part I to Part II. At first she appears as every other 'girlfriend' in an action film, but those twelve months that pass obviously change her as a person and I love the person she becomes: tougher, but still human."
   – Amber Moelter, actress, *Catwoman: Copycat*

"I finished *The Wraith* book last night. I must say I enjoyed it quite a bit. The scenes kept playing in my head like a big budget Hollywood film. I mentioned earlier that I enjoy when the hero is put to the test physically and doesn't win the battle unscathed. Boy, (Frank) delivered that in spades!"
   – Jeff Welborn, artist, *Nightmare World, The Wraith*

"Genius + sweat + dedication = hard hittin' hero action! Go Aussie!"
   – Dan Lennard, writer, *People* magazine

Praise for *Valley of Evil*

"The second Wraith novel is an improvement, I think. Right from the start Dirscherl throws you into the middle of crazy action.... This book is a whole lot of superheroic pulp fun, and the good news is there seems to be more to come...I look forward to some more of the same."

    – Richard Scott, *Super Reader* website

"I think (Dirscherl) really captured a noir element with (his) voice."

    – Joshua Gamon, writer, *Abigail & Rox, Digital Webbing Presents*

"I did quite enjoy the books. Best of all, it wasn't overly sex-filled or gory—I can't stand most modern superhero comics that show such things or have the heroes just swear and swear. So *The Wraith* (and *Valley of Evil*) was just up my alley."

    – Greg Gick, writer, *The Werewolf of Rutherford Grange, Tales of the Shadowmen, Secret Agent X Vol. 2*

"The Dread Avenger is back. After battling the Cobra in his first prose adventure, The Wraith returns to face all new challenges from Metro City's greatest villains, most notably Hong Kong drug kingpin Ma Tzi. As with his first Wraith novel, Frank Dirscherl treats us to a pulp-inspired adventure that keeps readers on the edge of their seat. You have to read this novel in one sitting."

    – Bobby Nash, writer, *Evil Ways, Fantastix, Lance Star*

"In the past five years there has been a tremendous resurgence in pulp fiction centering on the old heroic pulps. Young writers have started taking up the mantle of old masters like Walter Gibson and Lester Dent and begun creating their own avengers in tales of genuine purple prose. Among the best of this new generation of wordsmiths is Australian, Frank Dirscherl and the exploits of his modern pulp paladin, The Wraith. This is grand pulp!"
  – Ron Fortier, writer, *The Spider, Brother Bones, Domino Lady*

Praise for *Crossfire*

"Stephen did a fantastic job of bringing Frank Dirscherl's character to life!"
- Adam DiTroia, composer, *The Wraith: Eyes of Judgment*, MTV, Fox Sports

"Loved the book!! Can't wait for the next installment..."
- Larry Mainland, actor, *The Walking Dead, Lawless, The Three Stooges*

"The action comes swift, and doesn't stop until the final pages. *Crossfire* tells a great story of betrayal and revenge."
- C.R. Blevins, writer, *A Western Tale*

"This was my first introduction to The Wraith and I was not disappointed. The action comes swift, and doesn't stop until the final pages.... If you love a good action/hero story, you will certainly enjoy reading *Crossfire*."
- Ally, *Amazon*

"Makes me want more...should be the next series on Netflix..."
- Bill Lancaster, *Amazon*

"Another excellent entry in The Wraith Adventures series. Thoroughly recommended for Wraith fans and fans of pulp super-heroics."
- Leon Mallett, *Amazon*

Praise for *Cult of the Damned*

"Only by the first three pages, Frank Dirscherl wonderfully captures a dark and mysterious atmosphere, one that leaves the reader with a cryptic and eerie sensation; one that makes me cold just thinking about it."
> – Rennie Cowan, writer/director, *The Thriller Idol: A Tribute to the Legacy of Michael Jackson, Kade the Conqueror*

"Frank Dirscherl pulls you into the world of The Wraith from the first sentence and refuses to let you go until the last one."
> – Stephen J. Semones, writer/director, *Beyond the Lens, Crossfire, The Wraith: Eyes of Judgment*

"The Wraith is one of my favorite characters and every time Frank Dirscherl puts pen to paper I know I'm in for a real treat."
> – A.P. Fuchs, writer, *The Axiom-man Saga, The Way of the Fog, Undead World trilogy*

Praise for *Vendetta*

"...in all a great brew that had me hooked for the whole ride. Now bring on the next book, Frank..."

– Leon Mallett, *Amazon*

"This book starts with a literal bang and doesn't let the foot off of the gas until the very last page. The book is well plotted and moves at a breakneck pace, making it an enjoyable, short read. I loved this book very much as a fan of The Wraith and I believe that anyone who is a fan of the series should consider this required reading."

– Marcus Bucklin, *Amazon*

Praise for *Zombies Attack!* in *Metahumans vs the Undead*

"This compilation of superheroes vs evil offers top entertainment for superhero lovers! Frank Dirscherl and others are at their best with their contributed stories. I will now pursue other stories written by these authors, such as those involving Mr. Dirscherl's The Wraith. This type of reading enjoyment knows no end!"

–   Ramona Wingart, writer, *Where is Brother Beaver?*,
Emily Suzanne Smith!

Praise for *Werewolves Attack!* in *Metahumans vs Werewolves*

"Always a great read. Can never put it down once you get started... "

– Geraldine L. Lewis, Amazon

BY FRANK DIRSCHERL

FICTION

The Wraith Dread Avenger of the Underworld series

1. *The Wraith*
2. *Valley of Evil*
3. *Crossfire* (with Stephen J. Semones)
4. *Cult of the Damned*
5. *Cry of the Werewolf*
6. *Swamp Witch of Satan's Forest* (with Ray MacKay)
7. *Vendetta*
8. *Lady Wraith* (with Adam Oravec)
9. *Kingdom*
10. *City of Fear*
11. *Birds of the Living Dead* - COMING SOON

Books of Judgment

1. *Sanderson of Metro* (with Bobby Nash)
2. *Serpent Rising* (with Greg Gick)
3. *Rising Son* (with Adam Oravec) - COMING SOON

SHORT STORY COLLECTIONS

Metahumans vs. Robots
Metahumans vs. the Ultimate Evil
The Wraith Vol. 1
The Wraith Vol. 2 - COMING SOON
Lance Star – Sky Ranger Vol. 1

NON-FICTION

The Wraith: Eyes of Judgment – The Official Script Book & Movie Guide
(with Stephen J. Semones)
The Hitchers of Oz
Beyond the Lens (edited)

www.glowingeyesmedia.com

KINGDOM

The Wraith Dread Avenger of the Underworld #9

by

Frank Dirscherl

GLOWING EYES MEDIA
WOLLONGONG

GLOWING EYES MEDIA
PO Box 31
Wollongong NSW 2520

ISBN 978-0-646-72132-3

PUBLISHED BY GLOWING EYES MEDIA, July 2025
www.glowingeyesmedia.com
FRONT COVER ART by Anon
COVER LAYOUT AND DESIGN AND INTERIOR DESIGN by Frank Dirscherl
EDITED by AP Fuchs
FIRST EDITION

For more on *Kingdom*
visit www.glowingeyesmedia.com

Text set in Garamond-Normal. Printed and bound in the USA

NATIONAL
LIBRARY
OF AUSTRALIA

A catalogue record for this book is available from the National Library of Australia

The Wraith Dread Avenger of the Underworld series in correct reading order (including short stories)

So far...but the story goes on...

On the anniversary of your passing, this one's for you, Jim...

Jim Taylor
1963-2023

KINGDOM

~ Prologue ~

Paul Sanderson and his fiancée, Leena Patterson, were seated in the library of their city mansion, Sanderson House, enjoying a cup of coffee while discussing the ramifications of their recently-completed case. It had been a harrowing ordeal, one which they had barely survived.

"It's starting on the television now, sir," Simpson said, poking his head into the room.

"Hmm? Oh, thank you, Simpson," Paul said.

"Something on TV?" Leena said.

Paul nodded and reached for the remote on the table beside the coffee service. He flicked the switch and the large flatscreen television burst to life. "An announcement from Latham Industries."

Leena was perplexed. Even when Latham was alive it wasn't like him to appear on television like this. Interviews, yes, press conferences, occasionally, but public announcements? Unheard of. "What could this be about?"

"I doubt it's anything too important. Latham Industries is probably just announcing a new CEO to replace that fop Patrich Azufi. Or perhaps they're going under."

"Surely not," Leena replied.

Paul moved over and sat next to Leena, waiting for the announcement to commence.

"There, it's starting at last," she said.

Leena took another sip of her coffee and ruminated on the recent past. Over the past few months, Metro City had been largely devastated by the villain Crossfire, whose mad schemes of revenge saw the loss of countless lives, most notably those of crime lord Robert Latham, his erstwhile lackey Charlie Grieco, and Latham's possibly short-lived successor, Patrich Azufi did not get off scot free either. More recently, Paul had been kidnapped and the entire city embroiled in a nationwide conspiracy. It was almost too much to think about. And now, on this fine morning, something concerning Latham Industries. Leena would have rather been out and about on such a lovely, sunny day.

"Mayor Hutchison is about to speak," Paul said with a hint of surprise. "What does he have to do with Latham Industries?"

Leena looked on with intense interest.

"Ladies and gentlemen," Hutchison said into the camera in a stern voice, shifting his short, rubicund body somewhat uncomfortably, "as you know, this city has seen its fair share of tragedy in recent months. Gang violence, terrorist attacks, and, just last night, our city's finest conducted the largest arrest of its kind in this country's history. Prior to that, many innocent lives were lost, most notably my good friend and this city's patron, Robert Latham."

Paul snorted at that.

"Since his death, and the...incapacitation of his successor, Patrich Azufi..." Hutchison continued.

Incapacitation? Leena thought. *Since when?*

"...the company has naturally suffered. Its stock price has plummeted, offices have shuttered, jobs have been lost. And this city's fortunes have waned along with that of this fine company."

"He's laying it on thick," Paul said, rolling his eyes. "Even if the company is folding, it's hardly worthy of such a grandiose public declaration."

"However," Hutchison continued, his face brightening slightly, "amid all the doom and gloom, I can hereby announce there is hope. Hope for Metro City. Latham Industries is on the precipice of a new age of success and prosperity. Its destiny is to carry this great city forward along with it, as it always has in the past."

"Oh please," Paul blurted, rolling his eyes once again. Leena's thoughts mirrored Paul's.

"Only one person can guarantee such an outcome. Now" –Hutchison continued with his narrative, pausing briefly for effect, smiling the entire time– "this will no doubt come as a great shock to you all. It did to me only yesterday. But it has also brought me great joy...which I know you will all share with me. I am so very pleased to announce the CEO of Latham Industries, the man who is ready, willing and able to rescue the company, and the city as a whole–"

Paul sat upright, his eyes bulging. Leena turned from the TV to Paul and back again.

"–is actually its original CEO, its founder, and this city's great patron, Mr. Robert Latham!"

Leena couldn't believe what she was seeing or hearing. She was numb–and knew Paul would feel likewise–as though she was suffering from shock. She turned to Paul, whose jaw had almost crashed to the floor. He noted her expression then both returned their vision to the TV. There, on the screen in front of them, hobbling into frame, was indeed Robert Latham, their great nemesis. The man appeared older, somehow, and he needed a cane to walk, but the expression on his face–in his eyes–confirmed his identity at once.

The Wraith's enemy lived!

~ Chapter 1 ~

Cold trickles of sweat rolled down Paul's brow. His throat was suddenly parched in a way he hadn't experienced since his predecessor's time in the Eritrean desert. It was as though he couldn't move, frozen in time.

Is that a voice I hear?

"Darling? Paul! Snap out of it!"

Paul looked into her beautiful eyes and came back to himself. He returned his attention to the television.

"Mr. Latham will now explain his miraculous return himself," Hutchison concluded by way of introduction.

"Thank you, John," Latham said, his voice a little weaker yet still determined, the tone still sharp and cruel. "I stand before you a changed man. A humbled man. When that terrorist...Crossfire?" —he turned to Mayor Hutchison, who nodded in somber reply— "attacked me in my home, I managed to escape into a protective bunker in the basement. That quick-thinking saved my life, though the blast was so powerful, it nevertheless cost me my right leg." He tapped at the leg with his cane. It gave off a solid thud.

"Oh my," Leena uttered.

"But worse still, it cost me the life of my dear wife. Oh my darling." Latham bowed his head; tears welled in his eyes.

He almost looks authentic, Paul thought, then wondered if he was perhaps being too harsh on the man. Even Adolf Hitler loved his wife, after all.

Latham took the seat offered to him by the mayor and composed himself before continuing. "When I came to, I had no memory of who I was or how I came to have such catastrophic injuries. All I knew was I needed help if I was to survive. I managed to crawl from the wreckage of my home, used a plank to help me walk down to the street, where I flagged down a motorist, and...and..."

The crime lord choked up and appeared unable to continue his amazing story.

"It's all right," Hutchison said, stepping in and consoling his friend. "Ladies and gentlemen, Mr. Latham's office will be releasing a full statement to the press shortly, outlining the remainder of my good friend's story. I think we had better finish—"

"No," Latham said sharply. "No," he repeated, gently this time. "Allow me a few more words." He took a deep breath. "Suffice it to say, when I finally came to myself, I vowed to save this city. My wife often told me she was competing for my attention with this city. I used to laugh at that, but now...now I can perhaps see the truth in her words. I love this city. I always have. That...scum took my wife. I won't let him take my city as well."

Latham motioned to Hutchison and the press conference came to an end, a station announcer appearing onscreen to sum up what had just occurred.

Both Paul and Leena remained silent for moments that seemingly dragged on and on.

"Well," Leena said at last, "that proved to be more than either of us had expected."

"You have a brilliant way of understating things," Paul replied with more than a hint of sarcasm.

"He's back," she whispered.

"He's back."

* * * * * *

"Thank you, John," Latham said, taking Hutchison's hand in his and giving it a strong shake.

"Let me know if you need anything else from me," Hutchison said.

"I'll be in touch, rest assured."

And with that, Latham crawled into the back of his waiting limousine parked in the television studio parking lot and was soon off.

"Smithers, is it?" Latham enquired.

"Yes, sir," came the quick reply. "It's good to have you back, sir. This city will live again now that you're here."

"Yes indeed," Latham said, allowing himself the comfort of a wry smile.

Yes, my kingdom will rise again.

* * * * * *

Paul paced back and forth in the Lair, not really knowing what to think or do.

"Chief?"

"Hmm?" Paul said without much thought to whom he was speaking.

"Are you okay?" Max Horton said.

"Hmm?" Paul finally noticed the burly Irishman, who had been his right-hand man, his factotum, ever since he had tried to rob the original Paul Sanderson several years past in London. "Oh, Max. What is it you wanted?"

Max looked at him with some concern. "I asked if you were okay. And I don't think that you are. Is it Robert Latham?"

"As horrible as the man's murder was," Paul began while continuing to pace, "it nevertheless lifted a great weight from my shoulders. My greatest, most consistent enemy, gone. But today we find out it was little more than a dream."

A whirring of gears indicated an upstairs entry into the Lair. Leena appeared on the upper deck and, after descending in the micro-elevator, quickly joined them.

"I thought you'd be down here," she said to Paul.

"I'll tell you something," Paul said to Max, "I don't buy his coma story. Someone as well known in Metro as Robert Latham and the hospital he's in doesn't recognize him? Please. Something doesn't add up."

"You're right," Leena said, her face brightening. "There's no way we wouldn't have known of his survival before now, not if it all happened as he claims. What could he be up to?"

"Your guess is as good as mine," Paul said. "But it can't be good. And with this terrible drug epidemic in Metro at present...this is the last thing we need right now."

Leena and Max gave each other a knowing glance.

"Whatever Latham is planning...I have a feeling we won't have long to wait to find out."

* * * * * *

Patrich Azufi groaned as he awoke. He was momentarily confused. Everything completely foggy in his mind.

Where am I? What is this?

His head throbbed with the migraine of the century. He moved to grab at his head—but his right arm wouldn't budge. Panic gripped him. His entire body shuddered and the sweat began to flow.

What's going on? Why can't I move properly?

He looked about him. He was in a small, cramped bedroom. Very pink, very girly.

"Help!" Azufi screamed, almost involuntarily. "Help me!"

"Darling?" A sweet, feminine voice came from just outside the door. A gorgeous young lady appeared, long blonde hair, wearing a nurse's uniform. Curves in all the right places, her appearance in the open door brought it all back to Azufi. "It's all right, sweetie," Maggie-Grace Clifford, Azufi's nurse during his recent hospital stay, said, bending over and giving him a soft peck on the cheek. "Did you have another nightmare?"

"No," Azufi grunted. "I just...forgot where I was for a moment."

"Oh dear. Well, are you all right now? I really have to go to work."

"Must you?" Azufi said, almost pleading, which surprised him. "You know I hate being left alone."

"And you know I have to work," she said. "This apartment isn't cheap, and your disability check still hasn't turned up."

"Fine, fine," Azufi grumbled.

"Now, I've made you your breakfast already, just head into the kitchen and plonk yourself down," she said with a smile. "And, we'll have some *fun* tonight when I get home. I know you'll like that."

And with that, and a blown kiss, she was gone.

Azufi struggled to sit up in bed. His right arm was lame, a consequence of the explosion he and Maggie-Grace had been caught up in while heading for her car in the hospital parking lot. The fact he had convinced her to sneak him out of the hospital, with the intention of having sex at her place, is what saved his life that day. His voracious appetite was, in that case, his savior. The irony was not lost on him.

Nevertheless, the blast had caused him grievous injuries: damage to his spinal cord which left him partially paralyzed down his right side. He had tried continuing to work at Latham Industries, but he had found it extremely difficult to function at his best, then suddenly received word he'd been fired, the board having chosen another man, thus far unknown to him, to replace him.

The reality of his situation hit him once again–he was an invalid, disabled, good for nothing–being cared for, propped up, by a bimbo hick with no money and no future, living in a minuscule dump of an apartment.

But damn was she good in bed.

He tried to stand but his muscles ached and trembled in protest. He reached for his stick with his left hand, but fumbled with it, causing it to crash to the floor.

"Dammit!" Azufi cried out. "And damn you, Crossfire, for doing this to me. To *me*!"

He plopped down on the bed and gripped the bridge of his nose.

Damn it! I don't deserve this. I was a prince in this city once. Just moments ago. And now...now...

Now he had nothing. No wife, no home, no money. Fired from Latham Industries only a few days ago, the company was stalling over his compensation payout, so he was stuck here, with the bimbo in her hellhole.

It was then he realized just how attached he'd become to Maggie-Grace. Whether it was by necessity or true affection, he knew not. Regardless, he needed her. Truly needed her.

And damn was she good in bed.

~ Chapter 2 ~

"This is the thirteenth this month," Detective Bob Sloan, wearing his usual ensemble of T-shirt, jeans and baseball cap, grimaced as the coroner pulled the sheet over the young lady's head. The expression on the young victim's face had been horrifying. An eerie mixture of pain and anguish the likes of which Sloan had never seen before. And never wanted to see again. He felt guilty, as well. The recent pedophile case, and the overarching scandal, had prevented him from fully devoting himself to any other matter. And that galled him.

"All drug overdoses," his partner, Detective Rosa Perez, a pretty but plain young Latina who rarely wore much makeup, said in reply. "Some new drug on the scene? Or lethal new concoction? We don't normally get this many ODs in such a short space of time. And that look on her face..."

"Don't remind me, Perez," he said, scrunching up his nose. "But you're right: this is something new. All thirteen looked as she does. Heroin or Coke or Ice don't do that." He turned to the coroner. "Get samples over to the lab pronto. We need to know what we're dealing with and fast." He lifted his cap and put some fingers through his thinning locks. "Go call this in, Perez. Harrison will want to know about this."

She readily complied, exiting the room of the shabby apartment to make the call. Sloan pulled his cellphone from his pocket and started typing.

Another drug overdose. #13. Same symptoms as before. Definitely a new, deadly poison flooding this city. I'll have samples for you shortly.

A reply was quick in coming.

Good. This is now my top priority. We must identify this drug and halt its production and/or importation - W.

Sloan allowed himself a brief smile. He only hoped no more innocent lives would be lost.

* * * * * *

The Wraith crouched in the shadows atop a warehouse down by the waterfront. The ramshackle docks of this historic district, long since abandoned in favor of the larger, deeper waters of Barnett Bay some ten miles south, lay before him. The place was quiet and largely deserted, save for the occasional bum sauntering through on shaky feet.

He'd had a tip from one of his stoolies an undocumented vessel would be docking there tonight. He suspected it was the entry point for the deadly new drug currently flooding the city. It would end tonight.

Crime never rested in a city like Metro, with The Wraith constantly run ragged with every new emerging threat. But recent times had seen the city bedeviled as never before, what with Crossfire's war of vengeance, the gang war that had precipitated, and himself having been kidnapped and held prisoner. He really needed a break.

No sign of any vessel yet, The Wraith thought, scanning the area and out to sea with his night-vision lenses. He tapped at his right temple, increasing the magnification. Nothing. *No wait. There!*

In the murky distance, he caught sight of a medium-sized boat–larger than a fishing trawler, smaller than a tanker or cargo ship–sailing slowly toward the shore with only one narrow light extant.

This is it.

The quiet and largely abandoned area suddenly sprung to life, with two semi-trailers appearing to The Wraith's left and parking by Wharf Five.

It was time to make a move.

* * * * * *

"What are we carrying here, Phil?" the burly, ruddy-faced obese driver grunted as he gingerly stepped down from the cabin.

"How should I know, Red," his companion, a younger, beefier man, complained. "We're paid to do a job, so just shut up and do it."

They ambled over to the entry to Wharf Five and were soon joined by the driver and passenger of the other truck. They all muttered their greetings.

Moments later, an inky black sedan drew up beside them, its windows heavily tinted. It parked there for a minute in eerie silence before a rear door finally opened. A man in a charcoal suit and dark glasses emerged and approached the group, a tall, muscular bodyguard by his side.

"You gentleman ready?" the well-dressed man purred.

"What are we carrying, anyway?" Red blurted out. "It's late. I wanna get this over with."

The well-dressed man smiled, but it was a thin, steely grin, set in pursed lips and squinting eyes. "We are not here to make a delivery. We are here to pick up...cargo."

No sooner had those words been uttered, a vessel silently came into view through the fog and slowly inched into position alongside Wharf Five, ultimately berthing there.

"The authorities have been paid off and the area cordoned. There will be no interruptions while we load our precious cargo into the trucks," the man in the suit said with another steely grin.

Footsteps sounded at the far end of the wharf and, a few moments later, a parade of poor souls, chained by the wrists and ankles, shuffled their way forward, surrounded by men brandishing AK-47s.

"What...what's this?" Red sputtered. "This...this can't be what I think it is."

The man shot him a look. "And what do you think this is?"

Sweat poured from Red's brow. What had he gotten himself into? "I...I'll have no part of this. I need the money, sure, but this...this is too much."

He wanted to turn, to head back to his truck and get away as quickly as possible, but he hesitated long enough to see the well-dressed man nod subtly to his bodyguard, who produced a revolver from his coat and fired at Red.

That was the last thing he ever saw.

* * * * * *

"That takes care of that," the man with the high-end suit said. "Hurry up and get that filth over there into those trucks," he shouted. "Our client is paying top dollar for these slaves. This shipment is already delayed. We mustn't pause any longer."

The mix of Asian and Arab men were led to the rear of both trucks.

Not drugs but human trafficking, The Wraith ruminated from a safe vantage point, the reality of the situation sickening him to his stomach. *I've had enough of this crap recently to last a lifetime.*

"All right, all right," the man said. "Get them all inside, locked up, and ship them out."

As soon as the rear doors of each truck slammed shut, The Wraith struck, dropping from his position into the group of traffickers, his Eyes of Judgment crackling with fierce energy.

"Holy!" Phil cried.

"Filthy scum," The Wraith bemoaned, "now is your moment of judgment."

One of the armed boatmen, panicked, began firing indiscriminately. The Wraith leaped and rolled out of the way, only for several of the other armed men to fall all around him.

"Get him. Get him!" The man shrieked.

Swiftly, The Wraith lobbed a gas pellet at their feet; their confused shapes were almost instantly swallowed up by a billowing gray, acrid smoke. The Dread Avenger took the advantage, propelling himself into the fray, punching and kicking at each of his enemies with a pronounced ferocity. In minutes, all had been taken care of, save for Phil, the well-dressed man and the latter's bodyguard. Judgment was waiting for them.

"Stop him," the man shouted, pleading as much as anything else. "Don't let him get me."

The bodyguard fired with his high-powered revolver, catching Phil in the crossfire, who dropped to the cobblestoned ground like a lead balloon. The Wraith wrapped himself in his cloak, protecting himself from the barrage of bullets until the bodyguard's weapon was depleted.

In a lightning-fast move, The Wraith pulled his grapnel gun from his belt, aimed it at the bodyguard and fired. The grappling hook slammed into the bodyguard's right shoulder with a squelch of flesh and blood, causing the man to screech in agony. The Wraith yanked powerfully, bringing the bodyguard careening forward and into the path of The Wraith's powerful roundhouse punch, sending the bodyguard crashing into the side of one of the trucks and into a coma.

"Gotta get away," The Wraith heard the well-dressed man mutter, his upper-class accent suddenly slipping.

Backing up, the man managed to reach his sedan and scrambled inside.

* * * * * *

"C'mon, c'mon," he yelled as he tried to gun the Continental to life. But it was too late, for the cloaked demon with the strobing, yellow Eyes was upon him, crashing onto the car's hood.

The Wraith pulled something from his belt and fired, shattering the windshield into a thousand, dangerously-sharp pieces. The Dread Avenger reached forward, grabbed the man by the scruff and yanked him out. The Wraith's face was contorted in anger, teeth showing.

"Don't hurt me, don't hurt me," the man cried.

Police sirens blared in the distance and grew quickly louder. He would be saved from the demon's clutches.

The Wraith grunted, lashed out with a fist, and...

Darkness.

* * * * * *

"Well, well, what do we have here?" Sloan whistled as he led Perez and a cadre of police officers through the scene of the carnage by the entrance to Wharf Five. Unconscious bodies lay scattered everywhere as well as a few corpses.

"We have an injured man here," Perez cried out, "bleeding from a wound to the shoulder."

"Call an ambulance," Sloan ordered the officer alongside him, "though that punk doesn't deserve one."

Sloan and Perez moved over to the rear of one of the trucks and carefully pried it open. Terrified murmurs and sobbing, as well as a great stench, greeted them. Sloan shined a flashlight inside.

"Heaven help us," he said as they witnessed the pitiful sight before them. "He was right...human trafficking. So soon after the last case." He shook his head in utter exasperation.

The intense odor of sweat and lack of proper toileting caused Sloan to hack and wheeze. The fear-ridden, shackled innocents looked as though they hadn't eaten in a very long time. It was a clear miracle they had even survived their journey from wherever they had originated from.

"It's okay," Perez said gently to the group. "Nobody's going to hurt you anymore. We're here to help." Her soft voice did little to quell the fear still evident in their faces.

"I doubt they even know English," Sloan said. "Do we have any bolt cutters on site? Get more ambulances here on the double and call Human Services. Looks like we'll be pulling another all-nighter."

"Bob," Perez whispered, pulling her partner to one side, out of earshot of the others, "you said *he* earlier. *He* was right. You mean The Wraith, don't you?"

"He tipped me off about what was going on here tonight," he freely admitted, whispering in return.

She looked at him with incredulity. "Now you've got The Wraith's phone number? I don't believe this."

"I know, I know," he said, "but you yourself have always believed in The Wraith, supported what he's doing."

"Yes, but..."

"Well then? I trust him, Perez. Trust him with my life. End of story."

She sighed. "You know that's not the end of it, despite what I feel about The Wraith. You've been holding out on me, keeping things from me."

"Look, I'm sorry, but...you've been away for a while, remember? Things have...developed. You're just going to have to trust me on this one. *Trust* me. I can't say anything more right now."

The first ambulance arrived and Sloan moved over to direct their paths, eager to escape his partner's probing glare.

* * * * * *

"Wha...where am I?"

Before he knew what hit him, The Wraith grabbed the well-dressed man by the collar and jerked him up into the air.

"You'll be happy to know we're atop the city's tallest building," The Wraith grunted as his victim whimpered in abject terror.

"Wha...wha..."

"Who are you working for?" The Wraith said harshly through gritted teeth.

The man looked as though he was about to soil himself. "I...I...nobody."

"Who are you working for?" The Wraith repeated, louder, harsher, the Eyes of Judgment on his chest crackling into life. "In a moment, you'll willingly tell me everything."

"Okay, okay. I don't know his name. It's all arranged by text message. I'm just the small fry, you know?"

The Wraith pulled his victim close, their noses practically touching. "The way you dress, comport yourself, the phony accent. Your ride, your protection. You're no small fry."

The Dread Avenger lifted him up off his feet once again and carried him easily over to the edge of the rooftop, holding him out over the edge, a mighty three hundred-storey drop beneath. The man madly flailed about, panic setting in.

"Oh no, don't drop me, don't drop me!"

"Who are you working for?"

"I don't know," the man shrieked. "I was telling you the truth."

"You must know something," The Wraith spat with venom. "Tell me!"

"Okay, okay. Just don't...don't drop me."

The Wraith spun him around, launching him into the gravel.

"Talk," The Wraith ordered as he advanced on his prey, the Eyes of Judgment continuing to crackle with a fierce intensity.

"I don't know his name, all right," the man said as he attempted a crawled retreat. "Everything is arranged through middlemen, fronts, texts from fake numbers, that sort of thing. Money appears and we do what we're told, where and when." He managed to stand on shaky legs.

"I need more," The Wraith grunted.

"All I know is the word on the street...there's a big new player in town. Powerful, deadly, ruthless. Like a snake. He's gonna take us all down. This city, the whole country."

The Wraith growled in anger, let loose with a powerful right, sending the man to his knees. "Judgment is coming for your sins. Your soul will burn forevermore with the anguish you have caused others."

The Dread Avenger grabbed him by the head and bathed him with the energies of the Judgment Stare. A scream of horrific pain followed.

~ Chapter 3 ~

In the emergence of the dawn sun, Robert Latham's limousine cruised through the inner boroughs of Metro City. The crime lord gazed out his side window, inspecting the damage to his beloved city caused by that madman Crossfire. As the car journeyed on, the visible carnage became almost unbearable. The hospital, the police station, the airport, even his own corporate headquarters–all gone or substantially battered in Crossfire's insane quest for vengeance.

Latham eased back in his seat and sighed. He hurt, both mentally and physically. His leg ached, particularly at the point where his prosthetic met the flesh. He didn't need to heed the throbbing pain to know it was rubbed raw. And, ever since the blast that cost him both his leg–and the life of his dear wife–his head constantly pounded with pain and rang with a cacophony he'd been told he would have to live with the rest of his days.

"Damn you, Crossfire," he said under his breath. "Damn you for what you've taken from me. For what you've done to me."

"What was that, sir?" his driver called out.

"Nothing, Smithers," came Latham's terse reply. He gripped the bridge of his nose as he spoke. "I think we've seen enough now. I know what needs to be done to repair this city. Take me to the lab as originally scheduled."

Forty-five minutes later, through heavy traffic, the luxury car pulled up in front of a nondescript brownstone building. Along the length of this tree-lined avenue, the architecture of the buildings were reminiscent to similar such structures in New York City or San Francisco. However, the building Latham was now slowly approaching and was anything but a residential domicile.

They went through the front door, past a series of security guards, down a lengthy, shadowy lobby and into an elevator. A swipe of a pass card and Latham began a slow but steady descent. A few more minutes and he reached his destination. The elevator opened with a whooshing of gears to reveal a well-lit, expansive laboratory filled with equipment of all shapes and sizes and technicians and scientists by the dozen. It was a hive of intense activity; a buzz reverberated throughout the complex.

"Mr. Latham, sir," an extremely tall, cadaverous scientist with sunken Asian eyes and short, cropped jet-black hair, greeted with a smile. "We weren't expecting you today."

"Have you made any progress, Kai?" Latham pressed, ignoring the scientist's greeting. "I need that drug perfected. A drug that's one hundred percent fatal in even small doses is of no use to me."

"Daniel, sir," Daniel Kai replied. "Yes, we are making excellent progress with the Ophidium derivative. I feel we are on the cusp of a real breakthrough."

"Cusp!" Latham snapped, shuffling slightly on his prosthetic limb. "I need results *now*! Releasing the drug into a small section of the populace as a trial has shown its complete ineffectiveness." He gripped the bridge of his nose. "That fool Azufi ran my company into the ground. I need this drug perfected. This...Ophidium must be so patently addictive, and non-lethal except in extreme high dosages, that people will pay anything–*anything*–for another hit. The profits off this will be astronomical, especially as it will be created solely here in Metro City and not imported. Safer and more cost-effective."

Daniel Kai merely nodded, smiling while doing so.

"With those profits," Latham continued, "I can rebuild this city. My kingdom will be restored anew."

"Yes, sir," Kai said, his smile never leaving his face. "We will have results for you shortly, rest assured."

Latham snorted but said nothing more. He turned and gazed through the expanse of the complex. The funding of all this, the research, would all be worth it in the end.

My kingdom, he thought. *It will rise again soon.*

* * * * * *

It was early morning and ordinarily Paul Sanderson, after a long, hard night's work as the Dread Avenger of the Underworld, would be heading upstairs for a few hours of well-deserved sleep. Not today. Today, Paul just didn't feel like it. He was angry, frustrated, sickened by all he'd gone through in recent times. The pain and turmoil he'd seen, the depravity, weighed heavily upon him. There seemed no end in sight. He just wanted to hit something. Violence begets violence. He strode over to the Lair's fully equipped gym.

He removed his cowl, cape, and gloves and immediately set to work on the punching bag. There was no crescendo of violence as was the norm. This time he pounded with all his might right from the start. There was no thought behind it. Just raw, unadulterated violence. Blow after savage blow. Lefts and rights of unbelievable ferocity and speed. If the bag had been a human being...they would be long dead.

"Whoa, whoa," Max said, appearing as if from nowhere by Paul's side. "Steady on. That bag's not going to last, and neither will you if you keep up this intensity."

Paul shot Max a sideward glance then let loose with a mighty right. The bag tore loose from its overhead attachment, flew through the air, and slammed into the far wall. Dead and done.

"Chief, this isn't like you," Max said, his voice tinged with concern.

"I broke a human trafficking ring tonight, Max," Paul said after some moments of silence. "Broke," he scoffed. "In truth, I got nowhere. No word of who's truly behind this, no evidence of-"

"But you rescued all those people. Countless lives saved."

"But the person behind all this..." Paul said. "Someone powerful, deadly...like a snake..." His words echoed those he'd heard the night before, bringing forth an image of a man he dreaded thinking of.

"We've seen such horrors before, haven't we?" Max went on. "This is Metro City. Such horrors are a nightly occurrence."

"It isn't just that," Paul said, "it isn't just all we've been through recently. It's all that and more. This feeling sweeping over Metro. This sense of...doom, of..."

Max reached out and placed a hand on each of Paul's shoulders. "I know how you feel. In truth, I've felt it, too. So have others. It's a wave of...anxiety, perhaps, or depression, I don't know. I don't really yet know how to combat it. All I do know is we cannot give in to it. We have to persevere, stay strong."

Paul smiled weakly. He knew his friend was right and, in truth, both his workout and this little chat had somewhat cleared the air. Both had gotten things off his chest and shoulders. He almost felt himself again.

Almost.

"Now," Max started, "I've got work to do. Sloan sent that sample along. I have to determine what we're dealing with here."

Paul patted his friend on the arm. "Good. I'll head upstairs, get some rest."

A few minutes later, Paul had reached his bedroom, undressed and crawled into bed alongside Leena. As soon as he got comfortable she began snuggling.

"Hmm...long night?" she mumbled at least partially awake.

"Same as always," he said in a pointed tone. That did it.

Leena sat upright. "What's wrong?"

He knew better than to try and keep anything from her. "Human traffickers. And a deadly new threat, possibly whom Blackstorm was alluding to."

Leena gasped. "You mean..."

"Yes. I think he's back."

* * * * * *

Bob Sloan fell into a heap in his chair at police headquarters, thoroughly exhausted. He looked down at his desk through bleary eyes. Another all-nighter and here it was the following morning and he still had two extensive reports to write up. He wondered if he'd ever get home. He noted Perez taking a seat at her desk opposite his, looking as tired as he felt.

"Sloan, Perez!" a familiar voice cried out. "Get in here!"

Sloan and Perez exchanged glances before trudging over to Commissioner George Harrison's office. The door opened, they entered, and plopped down into their proffered seats.

"What's going on?" Harrison said. "A dozen bodies and now we have a human trafficking ring to deal with on the side. The city is still reeling from the pedophile scandal we just unearthed."

"You'll have a report on both within the hour, Commish," Sloan said.

"I know we're understaffed and under-resourced. I know morale is low, especially since we blew open the corruption within, both with the feds and in our own department. Taking all that into account, the mayor is still breathing down my neck. He and Latham plan on making some big announcement regarding their reconstruction plans, and these issues aren't helping the matter."

Sloan rolled his eyes. "Gimme a break. Crime doesn't take a back seat based on the mayor or Robert Latham's timetable."

"We're doing the best we can," Perez chimed in with a cliché that was nonetheless true.

Sloan knew well his partner had only just returned to duty, all the better for her rest, but was nevertheless still coming to terms with all that had occurred during her time away. To return to work, to the city itself, and be instantly thrust into such a vortex...Sloan hoped she was prepared for it all.

"I know you are, I know we're all in such an untenable position right now with all that's happened recently, but I also have to report to the mayor and try and justify all that we do." He sighed. Sloan saw the discomfort on Harrison's face. "Find me some perps and maybe we can all take a breather then."

With that, he motioned the conference was at an end, and Sloan and Perez stood, quickly returning to the squad room and their desks.

"He's a good man," Perez said, sitting down. "But the strain is starting to show."

"You're right," Sloan responded. "On both counts. With all the force has been through lately, with all this city has gone through...I can only imagine how Harrison is dealing with it all. He's been the rock that held us cops together all this time." He rifled his hand through his hair. "I'm heading to the lab. Maybe they've got something for us."

"Want me to come with?"

"No. If you could handle these reports, I'll owe you. Big time."

"Yeah, right," she said with a twinkle in her eye. "Get going, then."

As Sloan stood, collected his jacket from his chair and turned to leave, he hoped the police lab would have some news for him.

Some *good* news.

~ Chapter 4 ~

"I've got something, Chief."

Leena had long left for work and, sleep having eluded him, Paul had settled in the Sanderson House library alone with his thoughts.

Until now.

Paul pressed at the comm link on his nearby desk. "Yes, Max?"

"Ophidium," the Irishman replied.

Paul's eyes opened wide. Without another thought, he activated the library's secret entrance to the Lair and quickly plunged inside.

"Ophidium," Max repeated as Paul descended in the micro-elevator.

"Are you certain?" Paul said as he joined his comrade in the Lair's fully-equipped laboratory.

"Positive," Max said. "It's been altered at a cellular level, but there's enough of a footprint there to make identification possible."

"Altered?" Paul said, rubbing his chin. "Is that why it's proven so dangerous?"

"I'd say so."

"But why has it been altered? And by whom? Coyle? Or an ally of his?" Paul said. Coyle was the adversary they had previously encountered who had used Ophidium to deadly effect.

"No way of knowing," Max replied quickly. "Anything is possible." He stood from his microscope and straightened his back. "I can tell you this...whoever's been working on this has big ideas in train."

"How so?"

"Well," Max started, beginning to pace back and forth, "as far as I can determine, they're trying to remove the portion of the drug that transforms its victims into those...monsters–"

"I remember all too well," Paul said, briefly thinking back to the time they had last dealt with that insidious drug.

"–whilst maintaining that intense euphoric sensation that was a characteristic of the original drug."

Paul thought for a few moments. "A drug that kills almost instantly. Either someone is ready and willing to commit mass murder or..."

"The drug isn't perfected yet," Max said.

"I'm betting on the latter," Paul said. He started pacing the same time that Max ceased.

"This new, deadly player in town?"

Paul paced in brief silence before responding. "I don't think so. I don't think Ophidium and the human trafficking case are linked. No, drugs are more in Robert Latham's line, don't you agree?"

"Hmm...yes, perhaps you're right."

"This could be just the thing he's looking to do to revive his company's fortunes, especially if he's truly intent on helping this city rebuild. That sort of reconstruction requires money on a grand scale."

"Which means he has people working on perfecting Ophidium to maximize its addictive potential without killing its victims while maintaining its euphoric power," Max related.

"How much time do we have?" Paul queried. "Are they on the verge of a discovery?"

Max rubbed his chin, deep in thought. "Well, there's no way to be sure. The genetic manipulation here is on a genius level, and that requires time. I'd say they've been working on this for some period already."

"Pre-dating Latham's current travails," Paul murmured, more to himself than to anyone else.

"Right," Max added, "so releasing the Ophidium in its current state, to me, shows that whoever's behind this is in a hurry, trying to rush the project to fruition."

Paul nodded. To him, this affirmed his suspicion of it being Robert Latham behind the manufacturing and release of the drug. He continued pacing while Max remained silent in thought. After a few moments, he turned and headed back toward the elevator.

"Where are you going, Chief?"

"To see an old friend."

* * * * * *

"Sanderson," Latham greeted, his voice coarser but still retaining its familiar strength of character. Paul took the offered hand.

"Robert, you look..."

"Don't say well," Latham interjected. "I look like crap." He sat back down at his impressive mahogany desk as deep as a cricket pitch in his office located high within the Latham Industries building.

"I was going to say strong," Paul said. "You gave us all such a fright. It's good to see you back." He laid it on thick on purpose.

"I'm a tough sonuva bitch, that's for sure," Latham said with a slight smile.

He certainly was more candid and coarse than ever before, Paul thought. Latham also appeared...perhaps not quite haggard, but not far from it. He had lost substantial weight since Paul had last seen him, and his facial features were hardened somehow. There were more lines and his skin seemed almost...thicker, perhaps. His hair had also grayed to a great extent. Paul next eyed Latham's office. It was large and plush, with comfortably upholstered Sheraton chairs, a fireplace of Carrara marble, and artwork–prints?–by what appeared to be Constable and Sargent. Not the man's usual style, and the busts of the world dictators Latham so admired were nowhere in sight.

"I see you're admiring my new office," Latham said with a puff of his chest.

"Very nice, Robert," Paul said. "A little subdued for you, I would imagine."

"Not strictly my cup of tea, I agree," Latham countered, "but you know what...I'm kind of getting used to it. I originally intended this to be my temp office until my new one was ready but...now I'm not so sure."

"Oh yes, there must have been some significant damage here when–"

Latham held up a hand. Clearly, the thought of what had occurred wasn't something he wished to dwell upon. "Enough of all that. What's done is done." He shuffled some papers on his desk. "What are you here for, Sanderson? It's not just to shoot the breeze, surely."

"Well, I..."

"Ahh...I have it," Latham said after some thought, his face brightening. "You want to contribute to the city rebuild fund."

"Umm..."

"Now, don't hold back," Latham said, "I know you're almost as civic-minded as I am. Mayor Hutchison must have spilled the beans, the clever dog."

Mayor Hutchison? Paul thought. *Why does he think I've seen or spoken with him?*

"Well," Latham continued, "your contribution will be very welcome and no doubt do a world of good. This city needs all the help it can get."

"Of course," Paul replied, deciding it best to play along. "You know me too well, Robert. I'm only too happy to contribute to such a worthy cause."

"Good, good," Latham said, smiling broadly.

Somehow, it made the lines on Latham's face contort into fractured chasms, as though his had been pieced together like a botched jigsaw puzzle. The sight was unnerving.

"We can discuss figures later," Paul said as a way to end the discussion.

"Of course. My office will be in touch soon."

Paul looked down at his Erebus Ascent black enamel wristwatch, the new model in 36mm with the J-style steel bracelet. "I really must be going now, Robert. I have another appointment elsewhere." He stood.

"Good to see you, Sanderson," Latham said, rising slowly as though in some discomfort. "I won't see you out. Damn leg. As I said, my office will be in touch regarding your contribution."

"I look forward to it," Paul said, inching toward the door. "Good to see you in such fine fettle."

Latham sat back down gingerly as Paul exited the office and made his way down the lengthy hallway toward the elevators. As he walked, he looked about him. For the most part, you would never have known this building had been as extensively damaged as it had been during the Crossfire crisis. Everything was clean, painted, polished. More expensive-looking artwork lined the walls, pot plants were arranged at regular intervals.

That's money for you.

He also wondered what benefit, if any, his visit with Latham had been? What had he truly learned?

He's hard up for cash, that's for sure, Paul thought. *This building refurb would have been beyond expensive. And Latham would* never *have practically begged me for cash like that before. That and his prior narcotics connections and business make him the prime suspect in this Ophidium release. I can't let him perfect the drug. He has to be stopped.*

The Wraith will stop him.

* * * * * *

Ensconced within his Rolls Royce Wraith, Paul gunned the car out of the Latham Industries parking lot and into city traffic. As he navigated his way through the labyrinthian Metro streets, he ruminated over all that had occurred in recent weeks. The battles against Crossfire and the alien invader Trigoth. The formation of the Global Protectors. The pedophile ring and his kidnapping. All of it and more rumbled around in his brain, culminating in a dull ache throughout his cranium.

Coming back to himself, trying to shake the pain off, he noticed the grand Metro Cathedral looming into view up ahead. Its gothic architecture was a marvel of the city, if not the state, and it was where Leena wanted their wedding to take place. The thought of finally marrying the love of his life brought a wave of joy over him, washing the pain and harsh memories away. No date had yet been set, and with crisis after crisis bedeviling Metro City, he wondered when they would ever find the time for the ceremony.

Soon, Leena. Soon.

And there was the adoption hearing coming up as well. So much to do, so much...

No, Paul thought. *Focus. One thing at a time. Deal with the Ophidium situation, keep an eye on the human trafficking case and all else will follow from there.*

He collected his thoughts and steered the sports car past the cathedral, heading for home.

* * * * * *

The well-dressed man was now anything but, outfitted in a pale, prison gray uniform, seated in a cramped cell awaiting his visit before a judge. A lifetime of imprisonment beckoned. The joy.

It was dank and dark in his cell and now, once he allowed himself a break from wallowing in his misery, he noted how dark it truly was.

How odd.

There was also next-to-no noise, no talking, no crying out, no snoring...unheard of in a county lockup like this. It was almost as if the prison was largely...deserted?

Snap out of it, Troy, the man scolded himself. *Don't be stupid. It must be late, everyone's asleep. Yeah, that's it.*

He didn't really believe that, but what was the alternative? A sudden sense of dread and foreboding began to overwhelm him, and a wave of nausea settled in. He felt hot and clammy all at once and his throat became so dry he feared it might collapse in on itself. His breathing became labored. And then it happened–Footsteps.

Slow and heavy, they eerily echoed within the confines of the prison structure. Closer and closer. Louder and louder. Sweat oozed from every pore in his body. His hands shook. Troy squashed himself into the rear corner of his cell, yearning for escape from the nightmare that was no doubt coming.

A gigantic, shadowy form appeared before his cell. It was too dark to make anything out, but whoever it was was huge: a wardrobe on feet.

"You have failed me," a booming voice emanated from the shape. "I do not like failure."

"Wha...wha..." was all Troy could muster, his throat now utterly constricted, not that he truly knew what to say anyhow.

"You will be dealt with as I deal with all who fail me."

The shape reached for the cell door and yanked it from its hinges. Its right eye started to glow, emitting a strange, blueish hue. Then it started crackling with a fierce, electrical energy. Troy's bodily functions failed him. His final thoughts were of the strange, Cobra tattoo surrounding the shape's crackling right eye.

"It is over," the shape said.

Troy gurgled a pitiful attempted scream.
It was his last.

~ Chapter 5 ~

"**W**hat the hell is going on here, Perez?" Sloan said as they surveyed the scene within the county lockup. All the cells were filled with prisoners in a catatonic state, seated on their beds staring aimlessly out at nothing

All save one.

"Who is capable of doing this? And why?" Perez said.

Both were standing at the entrance to one cell in particular. Its door lay in the hallway, torn from its hinges. In the cell lay a body...or what was left of one.

"Torn apart," a CSI officer said, appearing by their side.

"You think?" Sloan retorted.

The CSI technician, garbed in traditional forensic gear, ignored Sloan's barb, pushed past the two detectives, and entered the cell. He examined the scene in silence for some time before speaking again.

"No evidence of any tools being used," he reported. "This appears to have been done by hand through sheer brute force."

Perez gasped.

"Where were the cops? Where were the guards?" Sloan said. "How could this happen with such ease?" He was upset. No, he was furious.

"Calm down, Bob," Perez said. "We'll get to the bottom of this."

"This shouldn't have happened at all," Sloan said as he turned and began to walk away. "This was the one man who could lead us to those behind the human trafficking ring."

"Troy Bramson," Perez read from her produced notebook. "We're still looking fully into his background. Nothing much of note so far." She tried following Sloan, who quickened his steps. "He was silenced, obviously. Knew too much."

"Sure, sure," Sloan said, never slackening his pace, as he made his way through the lockup. "But the power exhibited in there, the zombie hoods...why? How?"

"Bob, wait, stop."

He did and turned to face his exasperated partner. "There's something bigger behind all this, Perez. This isn't just human trafficking, this isn't just some rich people wanting cheap labor. No, something's going on here, something much more malevolent. More dangerous."

"What?" she said. "What are you saying? What do we do now?"

"I know what I'm going to do. You head back to the station. I have some thinking to do...and someone to see."

* * * * * *

The Wraith was perched atop the immense Metro Mutual Insurance building, his cape billowing in the night breeze, Metro City laid out before him like a mighty birthday cake ablaze with a million candles. The Latham Industries complex, ensnared in construction scaffolding, resembling an intricate spider's web as crews worked feverishly during daylight hours on the rebuild, was off to his right side.

In the dark, evidence of Crossfire's rampage was minimal at best and it was, The Wraith thought, when his city looked its best. Bright, shiny, almost clean. He wished it could always be thus.

Ideas of his next course of action snapped back at him. He was sure Latham was responsible for the recent drug epidemic. He had to stop him, of course, but how? What next?

His Herón Marinor wristwatch buzzed with word of an incoming message. He checked the dial–the indices flashed a vibrant orange. It was Sloan. The orange hue meant he wanted to meet.

Now.

* * * * * *

Sloan paced back and forth on the rooftop of Metro Police Plaza. The Wraith, hidden in the shadows, briefly watched him, noted his dour expression--the detective's muscles were tensed and taut.

"What is it, Sloan?" The Wraith said, stepping forth from the darkness. "What was so important we needed to meet?"

"Troy Bramson was murdered last night," Sloan said, without preamble.

"Who?" The Wraith said, perhaps a little more sharply than he ordinarily would.

"The human trafficking case, the guy you bagged the other night."

The well-dressed man.

"Ripped apart," Sloan continued, "mutilated by hand by someone of immense strength."

The Wraith couldn't believe what he was hearing. Their one link to the case gone in a violent assault.

"The other prisoners in the lockup were left in a catatonic state. We still can't revive them. Guards went AWOL during the attack. Bought and paid for, no doubt. All have been fired, pending investigation."

The Dread Avenger was stunned into silence. He pondered these facts with great concern. Everything was leading back to the one source, every piece of the puzzle leading back to the one man–Blackstorm's origins, Troy Bramson's confession, the comatose prisoners in the county lockup. All of it pointed in only one direction–the Cobra.

"Someone is coming, Sloan," The Wraith said. "Be prepared. Get everyone ready."

Sloan's eyes bulged open.

"Death is coming."

* * * * * *

"He's here? Wants to talk to me at this hour?" Latham, speaking into his intercom, was incredulous. "Fine, send him in."

After a long few minutes, Patrich Azufi shuffled into Latham's office, looking the worse for wear after his recent ordeals. Latham could sympathize...if he actually cared.

"What are you doing here, Azufi?" Latham said seated at his desk. "We've said all we have to say to each other. Your phone call yesterday was the last straw as far as I'm concerned. The rest is up to our lawyers."

"Listen here, old man," Azufi demanded, waving a crutch at Latham, "you owe me. I did everything you told me to do without fail. I took care of this company while you were...gone, kept things afloat during difficult times. And what reward do I get? What thanks? Termination!"

Latham remained calm despite an explosive fury welling inside him. "Are you finished?" He shuffled some papers on his desk, his latest go-to delay tactic. "You kept my company afloat? Are you trying to be funny?"

"Times were...*are*...tough," Azufi said, clearly losing his composure, the veneer of strength and confidence rapidly slipping. "You were gone, this company faced barrage after barrage, rampant inflation. No one could have done better under the circumstances."

Latham shot to his feet faster than even he thought under his current circumstances. He couldn't hold his anger any longer.

"You arrogant fool!" Latham shouted. "You allowed yourself to be taken in by that brutish oaf Crossfire. You let him get away with mad scheme after mad scheme. And it almost destroyed what I'd spent a lifetime building from scratch. You bastard!"

Latham then allowed himself a broad smile as Azufi watched on in confusion.

"What are you smiling at, old man?" Azufi ultimately said, trying vainly to regain the upper hand or, at least, some semblance of strength of character. He failed.

The door to Latham's office swung open, revealing three broad-shouldered men outfitted in splendid Italian tailored suits, their jackets open, revealing a firearm strapped to each of their sides.

"You alerted your thugs," Azufi shrieked. "You coward. Can't deal with the truth, trying to deny me my just reward."

Latham grunted at that. "Oh, my men here will ensure you get your *just reward.*"

The three guards grabbed Azufi and began dragging him from the room. "Nothing you do to me will deny the truth. I want what's coming to me."

As Azufi was removed from the office, kicking and screaming the entire time, Latham cried out, "You'll be getting what's coming to you, I promise you. Whether you survive it or not, I'll leave that up to my men."

The conference was over. Latham had always enjoyed wielding the power that was rightfully his, exerting it, using it to decide who lived or died. And that was partially true this time as well, however...the entire incident nevertheless left an acrid taste in his mouth. He sat back down and wondered if he was somehow losing his thirst for power, or if his injuries had weakened his character in the same way it had his body. He had no immediate answers and ultimately shrugged the notion off.

His injuries, and his recovery to that point, had taken too much of his energy, too much of his attention, he finally decided, and he had thus far had no time to devote to rest and relaxation. There was no time, in truth, for such, not with his empire on the precipice of crumbling around him. No, rest would come later once his kingdom had been fully restored and his power returned and consolidated. Then, and only then, would he allow himself some reprieve.

In the meantime, he had work to do.

* * * * * *

The heavy metal door to the back alley at the rear of the Latham Industries structure burst open and Azufi was tossed aside as though a pile of garbage, landing heavily amongst the trash and filth.

"You'll pay for this," Azufi shrieked. "When I reclaim my power, you'll all pay."

Each of the three guards looked to each other in turn and smirked. One reached for his piece, holding it aloft. Another raised his hands and cracked his knuckles.

"I'm gonna enjoy this," the knuckle guard said.

He stepped forth, reached down and yanked his hapless victim aloft as though he was a child's toy. He thrust him against the adjacent wall, face first, and pummeled his fists into Azufi's kidney's. The former crime lord cried out in pain and quickly sank to the ground.

The guard with his gun in his hand then joined in, sending his boot into Azufi's abdomen one after the other. Soon, a crack was heard and Azufi cried out again. He was sure he was done for. There was no way he was getting out of this one.

With what he thought was his last breath, his final moments, he wanted to look his assassins in the eyes, make them feel their crime as much as he could. So he forced his eyes open, strained his battered body around to face his attackers. He hacked up a volume of bloody sputum but held his gaze on his killers.

He saw and felt a gun being rammed into his forehead...and he knew it was all over. Darkness was looming and, perhaps, blessed death?

"Judgment is at hand!" a deep, resonant voice boomed.

In the seconds Azufi had before unconsciousness overwhelmed him, he could have sworn he saw something glowing, something...terrifying.

Darkness.

* * * * * *

The Wraith dropped as though from nowhere right in between the three attackers, forcing them back on their haunches.

"Hey!" one shouted.

"What the...?" another said.

"Your days of preying on the innocent are over," The Wraith moaned. "Now you will be judged."

The thug with the gun proved quick on his feet. He had his gun raised and fired off a round in two quick beats, almost catching The Wraith by surprise. He managed to wrap his protective cloak around him, allowing the bullets to ricochet safely away.

In an instant, he lunged at the thug, grabbed and disarmed him, then hurled him into an adjacent dumpster. The other two thugs attacked in unison, one on each side of the Dread Avenger. He saw it coming, lashing out with a right to the nose, then swung around and delivered a powerful uppercut to the other. The shattering of teeth reverberated throughout their confined space. He was out for the count.

"You...bwoke my...dose," the remaining thug wailed, trying to stem the flow of gushing down his face.

The Wraith had no intention of taking pity on his enemy, quickly lashing out with a side kick to the head, sending this thug into a peaceful, albeit painful, sleep.

Thinking the situation dealt with, The Wraith relaxed ever-so-slightly. It was enough of a slip to be caught off guard by the thug emerging from the nearby dumpster, brandishing a second firearm The Wraith knew nothing about. The thug fired from close range. Despite this, The Wraith managed to maneuver his body just enough so the bullet merely caught him a glancing blow to the right shoulder, his uniform protecting him from the brunt of the blast.

"Now you will face judgment for your sins," The Wraith uttered, "and your soul will be cleansed."

The thug never knew what hit him. The Wraith reached for his assailant's head, jerked it down toward the crackling Eyes of Judgment, and bathed the hapless man in the mystical energies of the Judgment Stare. All the thug could do was scream. Then he collapsed in a writhing heap, forever a changed man.

The Wraith allowed himself a brief moment to catch his breath, then rushed over to the prone man who had proven the cause of this melée. He checked for a pulse...the man lived...but barely. His heartrate felt weak. It was then The Wraith recognized who it was–Patrich Azufi. He gasped a little at the realization, saw how grave Azufi's wounds were. He wondered if the erstwhile crime lord would survive.

The Wraith tapped at his temple. "Emergency evac, Max. We have a man down. It's Azufi, gravely injured, in need of immediate attention. Call it in."

"Aye, Chief," came the almost-instant response.

Emergency personnel would be there shortly. Azufi's survival was now in their hands. The Wraith wondered what had brought all this on. He decided this was not the place for such pondering, however, and produced his grapnel gun from his belt. He pointed it skyward and was soon up and away.

~ Chapter 6 ~

Azufi came to with a jolt and found himself in a hospital room. Again. As woozy and doped up to his eyeballs as he was, he cursed his abominable fortune. To have once been the prince–nay, the king–of Metro City, only to be turfed from the heights of glory a mere few moments later through no fault of his own. No, they were out to get him. They were all out to get him.

"Oh darling," a sickly sweet voice rang out.

It was Maggie-Grace, his new paramour, and the one who was now taking care of him like a child.

"My darling, what happened? What did they do to you?"

Her voice annoyed the heck out of him, all girly and sweet as treacle, but she was definitely hot, especially in her nurse's uniform. Still, the fact that such a bimbo was now his savior galled him to no end.

"Will...will I...be all right?" Azufi struggled to speak. Whether it was the drugs he was on or through his injuries, he knew not. All he knew was he couldn't move and could barely talk.

"You're badly hurt," Maggie-Grace said with much concern. "Broken ribs, ruptured spleen, heavily bruised kidney's, a range of contusions...but you'll live."

In his current state, he wasn't sure if that was a good or a bad thing. Perhaps he was better off dead. What future did he have now? His career and reputation in tatters, his fortune dwindled, virtually homeless. All he had left was this angelic form standing before him. A wave of gratitude and revulsion engulfed him all at once, confused him, enraged him.

Perhaps he *was* better off dead.

* * * * * *

Daniel Kai stood erect, staring intently at his oversized computer monitor. He was perplexed by what he saw. On it were images of the Ophidium drug: its microscopic structure, the genetic enhancements he instituted. He reached forward, manipulated the imagery, turned it round and round, viewing it closely from every angle. He just couldn't understand why the drug wasn't working as it should. He'd tweaked the genetic code, removed the portion of the drug that proved so lethal to all its introduced subjects. He'd protected and increased the portion of the drug that controlled its pleasurable and addictive effects. All should be working as ordered. So why wasn't it?

What am I missing here? Kai went over and over the problem in his mind.

Both on the screen before him and in his mind's eye, everything was perfect. He saw nothing out of place, nothing that hadn't been altered that should have been. And yet, the Ophidium was still, as of earlier today, absolutely useless. As soon as a subject imbibes in their chosen fashion, after a few moments of incredible ecstasy, they die a horrific–albeit pleasurable–death.

Why can't I get this to work? Why? What am I missing here?

He rotated the imagery on his screen again and again, probing for any minute detail he had previously overlooked, as unlikely as he knew that to be. But he needed answers and, so far, he was unable–incapable–of finding any. And that frustrated him. Infuriated him. Worried him.

As he continued to ponder his complex problem, the phone at his desk buzzed. He briefly considered ignoring it, then thought better of it. He answered reluctantly.

"Yes," Kai snapped. A moment later: "Oh, Mr Latham, sir. My apologies, I was deep in study on our current...problem, and I did not wish to be disturbed. Yes, sir, my apologies again, sir."

He had to control his emotions. Robert Latham was his benefactor; none of his myriad projects would be possible without the infusion of funds from the city's great entrepreneur.

"Yes, sir, I understand. I will have results within the next day or so. I will let you know the instant it occurs."

He hung up and took a deep breath then a swig of water from the glass on his desk. He worried he was making promises he no longer able to keep.

He shook his head. Was he not the preeminent microbiologist and physicist in the country? Nay, the world? DNA and even subatomic particles were but mere playthings to him, to be manipulated and altered at will. He'd worked on hundreds of projects for various governments of the world, creating countless viruses, poisons, even creatures to be used in possible future conflicts. He had never failed at an assignment. Never. And yet...

He returned to the problem at hand. Finally, he took a seat at his desk, and eyed his computer monitor intently.

The solution must be here somewhere, he thought. *I will not rest until I find it. Failure is no longer an option.*

Robert Latham would see to that.

* * * * * *

The Wraith sat at his desk in his Lair, contemplating his next move. Should he confront Latham head on, demanding answers? Should he tail Latham, become as one with his shadow, tracking his every move? Should he infiltrate his organization in disguise, discovering the truth that way?

Why was it so difficult to ascertain his next move? Normally he was so sure of himself, never doubted, always knew the next course of action. Had he been more mentally wounded by his recent kidnapping ordeal than he had originally thought? Or had the citywide dark mood afflicting many started affecting him as well? In that moment, he just wasn't sure. He wasn't sure of anything.

Ultimately, he snapped back to the task at hand and shrugged all the available options away. No, Latham would be smarter than that. And he was immune to his threats, even to his Judgment Stare alas. No, this situation required a different approach.

He just wasn't sure what that approach would be.

* * * * * *

Could this be the answer?

Daniel Kai broke out into a broad smile. He'd been racking his brain all night and now into the morning. He had discovered that, despite all his perfect genetic tampering, somehow, on a subatomic level, the slightest of strands of the Ophidium's DNA was fracturing. It was only discernible at the very highest possible magnification. He doubted any other scientist on the planet could have discovered it.

So, the problem had been identified. Next came the solution. For hours, nothing became evident. Then, in a moment he saw as sheer genius, a provocative idea flashed into his mind–linking the deadly poison Xycosin to the Ophidium's genetic code. Just a tiny portion of it, the merest fraction, but Xycosin's inherent stability might, just might, bind the Ophidium's DNA in a way that allowed it to work as programmed. He just had to remove the component within Xycosin that made it so deadly. That was the easy part. Linking it to the Ophidium, ensuring the bind was strong and in the correct percentile range...that was the harder part.

Hard but not impossible.

Nevertheless, he firmly believed he was onto something, and he hadn't a moment to waste. He briefly wondered where such an idea had sprung from but quickly swept the notion away. Genius was often inexplicable. He jumped to his feet and raced down the corridor, heading for the lab's extensive storage facility. He was sure they had at least a small sample of Xycosin on hand.

That would be more than enough.

* * * * * *

Paul and Leena sat beside each other in the back of their classic Daimler sedan, Max piloting the car through the busy city traffic. Both were outfitted in their finest–Paul in a superb bespoke tailored charcoal suit from his tailors at Cad & the Dandy, while Leena wore an elegant gown from her favorite designer, Alex Perry.

"Well, that went rather well, I thought," Leena said.

"It did," Paul replied. "My attorneys think it's a foregone conclusion."

"What does that mean, exactly?" she said.

"It means," he said, "that once all the forms are submitted, a final interview or two conducted, some requisite fees paid, and Emily could be with us within the month."

"That's wonderful," Leena said, a smile forming. "It's so exciting and such a big change for us."

"One we're ready for, I think. Some adjustment, sure, but no different to any other expectant parents."

"Except this child is six years old," Leena said.

"The principle is the same," Paul said with a grin.

The remainder of the ride home was spent in pensive silence. He was beyond happy at the developments in his personal life. Engaged to the love of his life, adopting a beautiful little girl. But the other side of his world, the one inhabited by the Dread Avenger, was in turmoil, as it almost always was. Thirteen victims of some new drug–Ophidium, Max said–human trafficking rearing its ugly head again and the possible return of his deadliest enemy ever.

As Max pulled the car into the lengthy Sanderson House driveway, Leena sat forward.

"You've gone awfully quiet," she said.

"Hmm...oh sorry, darling. I was just thinking."

"Of what? Or should I ask?"

"I'm sure you can guess. The cases we're working on right now, the potential ramifications involved. With everything that's going on, it's hard to keep it all together."

"Ramifications...you mean the Cobra? You really think he's back? That he survived that fall?"

Paul sighed, gripped the bridge of his nose. "Yes, I think he did. We have to be prepared."

~ Chapter 7 ~

Daniel Kai shrieked with joy. "Success!" His surrounding subordinates barely roused themselves from their own duties, no doubt thoroughly accustomed to the scientist's bizarre behavior.

I've done it, Kai ruminated. *The bind between the Xycosin and Ophidium is secure.*

No more degradation of the drug's DNA at the cellular level, just as he had surmised. But would the Ophidium work as instructed? As it needed to? There was a possibility, slim perhaps, it would not work at all, or at least not exactly as desired. Further tests were needed to determine the new drug's efficacy. Either way, he had to let his generous benefactor know of his latest results.

Kai took a seat at his desk and was about to reach for his phone when he heard some little commotion at his rear.

"Kai!"

He recognized the voice.

"Mr. Latham, sir," Kai said, bowing slightly. "I was just about to telephone you."

"I hope that means you finally have good news for me," Latham said, clearly agitated as he walked slowly forward.

"I do indeed," Kai said. "I have rectified the inherent flaw in the genetically modified Ophidium–"

"Does this mean it will now work?" Latham said, cutting Kai off. "As it should?"

"I believe so. I hope so."

"I want this finalized now!" Latham said. "Test it. Release the drug to a select group as before."

"In the wild? But Mr. Latham, sir...there could be repercussions. If it does not work as planned, or perhaps..."

"Enough!" Latham snapped. "I need this settled. Get it done. Report the results to me." He grunted and turned to leave, then stopped. "The crackhouse on Fifth. Report to me your findings." With another grunt, he began his arduous journey for the exit.

Well, there was the answer. We move on to the testing phase. Immediately.

There was some trepidation. He was supremely confident in his own abilities, in his own judgment, but he would ordinarily take things a little slower, even in his own field of...questionable science. At least that was the way the regular scientific community looked upon his work prior to his retreating from society and establishing his more underground scientific endeavors. Since coming under Robert Latham's benevolence, the scope of his research had broadened immensely. He was now investigating molecular structures, genetic splicing, the fertility of every known creature...even combinations of all of the above. And more. It was wonderfully exciting to push–shatter–the boundaries of science.

Creating a new drug for Latham was, he readily admitted, more on the mundane side of his recent technological forays, but then the crime lord was paying the bills so who was he to argue? He had made some real, genuine scientific breakthroughs, so what did he care about others' potential suffering? The strides in understanding achieved outweighed all else.

The crackhouse on Fifth. Time to get started.

* * * * * *

"Dammit, I want answers!"

Harrison wasn't pulling any punches, letting both Sloan and Perez know of his fury at the recent events at the county lockup.

"Corruption, Commissioner, pure and simple," Sloan said, retaining his composure. He'd seen it all before. "No matter how well we've done in cleaning up the place over the years...it's never enough."

"But, who?" Harrison said. "Who's behind all this?"

"Robert Latham, surely, is the only one who comes to mind," Perez said, pointing out the obvious.

"To what end?" Sloan said. "You think he's involved in this human trafficking enterprise?"

"Or the head of it," she said. "Why not? He has his hand in everything rotten in Metro."

Ordinarily, Sloan would agree with her. Latham was, and always had been, the giant insidious spider located at the center of all Metro's web of crime. But, after what The Wraith told him recently...he now felt differently.

"I don't know, Perez."

"I don't care if it's Latham or someone else," Harrison boomed. "I want them found and brought to justice. Yesterday!"

Sloan looked over to his partner and raised an eyebrow. She returned his glance with clear understanding. Neither said another word. Sloan nodded to Harrison, and both quickly retreated from the commissioner's office.

Walking down the hallway back to their desks, Sloan rubbed his head. "Good luck nailing Latham on this, if he's responsible. Like we've been able to get anything concrete on him after all these years."

"What's this *if*!" Perez said. "You doubt Latham's involvement in this? Who else could it be? Who else has that level of power, or reach, in this city?"

"Perez, I..."

"Hang on just a minute," she said, stopping Sloan in his tracks. "You've got some actual intel on this. You *know* it's not Latham, don't you? You've spoken with The Wraith."

"Keep your voice down," Sloan whispered, grabbing her by the arm and escorting her back to their desks. "I don't know who it was. I have nothing concrete. I just know it wasn't Latham."

Perez's eyes bulged at the revelation but she remained quiet for a few moments. They both plopped down in their chairs. Finally: "It's morning...what's our next move then?"

Sloan leaned back, furrowed his brow. "I'll let you know when I work it out for myself."

* * * * * *

Paul awoke in his sumptuous bedroom suite to find Leena dressing for work. She exited their walk-in robe with a smile on her face.

"I wasn't going to wake you," she said. "I know the stress you've been under. I thought you could do with the rest."

"I got a couple hours," Paul replied. "Sleep isn't that easy to come by lately."

He sat up in bed and Leena dropped down beside him. "Anything I can do?"

"Nothing right now. I think The Wraith will have to pay Robert Latham a visit tonight."

"What will that achieve?" Leena's eyes were filled with concern.

"Maybe nothing," he said. "My hope is, with what Latham has gone through recently, he'll slip, make a mistake, perhaps leave some sort of clue..." He wanted to say more but his voice trailed off.

"Not likely."

Paul sighed. "I have to do something."

Leena made to reply but stopped short at a strange sound coming from the bedroom door. Make that *sounds*. Something like scratching and...whispering?

Paul put a finger to his lips, carefully slid out of bed, and headed for the almost-closed door. Tiptoeing, he flung the door open to reveal...Max standing awkwardly before him.

"Max?" Paul said.

"Chief, I was just...uh...uh...talking to myself...about the case," Max said, not entirely convincingly.

"Are you okay, Max?" Leena chimed in, now standing alongside Paul.

"Fine, fine," the Irishman said. "I'll be in the Lair." He stomped down the upstairs hallway.

Leena stuck her head out the door and watched Max turn the corner, heading toward the stairs. Paul quickly joined her.

"What was that all about?" Leena said.

"Hmm..." was all Paul could say in reply.

Leena took a peak at her Rolex Oyster Perpetual wristwatch. "I better hurry. Big meeting at work this morning."

"Anything interesting?"

"Not really," she said. "Some talk of a staff restructure in the library. Management brings this up every couple years or so. Usually leads nowhere. But I have to argue my case against it, as I always do."

Paul knew all about that and he knew it was an unwise person who would argue against his fiancée over something she passionately believed in. That was a no-win situation for any poor soul who tried it. Whatever issues there may have been within the city council, or the library itself, the library staff was not part of the problem.

"Will you be home for dinner?"

"Are you cooking?" Leena said playfully.

Paul shook his head no.

"Then I'll be home on time," Leena said with a giggle. She gave Paul a kiss then plunged out into the hall.

Paul ruffled his hands through his hair. What an odd morning. He wondered if he should press Max on...whatever that was. Having showered before coming to bed earlier that morning, he entered the wardrobe, and ultimately thought against talking with Max. After all their experiences recently, a little strange behavior was surely forgivable. In moments, he was outfitted in khaki chinos and a navy Sunspel Riviera polo shirt. The perfect casual ensemble. Then over to the built-in watch winder, which held almost all his watches—the Héron Marinor, his Erebus Ascent and his Jaegre Le Coultré

Reverso, having discarded all his other watches in recent times, save for the Rolex Submariner the original Paul Sanderson owned and which was located in the Lair. He again chose his Erebus Ascent and, moments later, descended the staircase.

"Mr. Sanderson, sir," Simpson said, greeting him at the foot of the stairs, "would you care for your morning repast?"

"Just coffee, thanks."

Simpson did not appear pleased. "You need some nourishment, sir. I'm afraid I'm going to have to–"

"Fine," Paul said, raising his hands in surrender, "fine. My usual then."

Simpson smiled–a rare occurrence–and was off.

"Simpson, before you go..."

"Yes, sir?"

"Have you noticed anything...wrong with Max? He seems a bit...off this morning." Paul didn't know how else to describe it.

"Off, sir?" the butler replied. "I can't say that I have noticed anything peculiar with Master Max, although I have not seen him since yesterday. Is that all, sir?"

"Yes, thank you, Simpson."

"Very well, sir. I shall have your breakfast ready for you shortly in the breakfast room."

Paul made his way there and poured himself a cup of the finest Vittoria coffee from the steaming pot waiting for him. He took a seat in the nook and ruminated over what his next course of action would be.

I know Leena's right, but I fear I may still have to try it. Robert Latham will be seeing The Wraith–tonight.

* * * * * *

"There you go, Patrich. You rest here a bit." Maggie-Grace patted him on the head.

"Stop handling me," Azufi barked.

He was extremely agitated. Beaten, humiliated, and now was being treated like a petulant toddler, at least to his way of thinking.

"Patrich," Maggie-Grace said, pouting. "You need rest. You've been badly hurt. Now lie down in bed." She was doing her best matron impersonation. It helped she was in her nurse's uniform.

"Stop pestering me! Can't you just leave me alone?"

"Well," Maggie-Grace said, her pouting increasing, "if you're going to be that way." She turned to exit the bedroom.

"Maggie-Grace, wait," Azufi said, surprising himself. What was going on?

"Yes, Patrich?" she said, turning her head.

"Please don't go," Azufi said, continuing to surprise himself. Where were these words coming from? "I need you."

Maggie-Grace melted at his words. "Oh Patrich." She moved over to him, took him in a bear-hug that was, perhaps, a little too rough. "Everything will be all right, you'll see. You just need to rest and heal."

Azufi did as he was told and lay down on the garish pink bed. "Okay. I could do with a nap."

Maggie-Grace stood, smiled and eyed him lovingly. "I'll be in the front room. I'll make dinner in an hour. You take your nap."

Azufi closed his eyes at her exit. As he lacked insurance, he was deemed healthy enough to leave the hospital early. Healthy? What a joke. He felt half-dead. Then, another thought hit him like a sledgehammer, and he opened his eyes suddenly.

I need you? Where the hell did that come from? I must be losing it. This bimbo means nothing to me. And yet...

He sighed. He didn't know what to think. And that concerned him.

A lot.

* * * * * *

Daniel Kai almost collapsed into his chair back at his lab. It was now early evening and he'd spent all day behind the scenes ensuring the new Ophidium was ready and distributed to the various guinea pigs on hand at the nominated location on Fifth Avenue. There were plenty of fools available for a qualitative study. Initial reactions observed were extremely encouraging–instant exultation followed by a consistent sense of mellow sanguinity. No detectable adverse response. The drug would, naturally, be impossible to resist, no matter how slight the dosage. He had seen to that. All proceeded as planned.

Despite his immense joy, he was exhausted. He'd been at it constantly for days. Weeks, really, ever since Robert Latham had somehow found him in his secret, somewhat austere location. He had been down to his last few dollars when the crime lord had offered him a deal he could not refuse. He'd been putting in twenty-plus-hour days ever since. Now he had succeeded beyond even his wildest imaginations. The riches would flow his way accordingly. Tired as he was, he couldn't help but smile. The smile turned into a low chuckle then a high-pitched cackle. None of his colleagues even turned an eye.

Before he could rest, take in all his accomplishments, Kai had to inform Latham of his great success. Basking in his glory was part of the fun after all. He reached for the phone.

"Mr. Latham, sir," he said. "Great news. The test was successful. All outcomes were achieved. No casualties." A moment. "Oh, thank you, sir. Your patronage is most appreciated. I shall always endeavor to do my best for you." He beamed at the reply then hung up.

Success was such a high for him. Almost as much as the Ophidium was to the gutter-trash of Metro City. He giggled at that. He preferred the healthy route to ecstasy rather than tripping.

* * * * * *

A cold night wind sliced through the various alleys of Metro like a hot knife through butter, piercing the almost non-existent items of clothing on the plethora of homeless ensconced throughout. As the weather turned more icy and the wind became more blustery, it quickly proved too dangerous for the usual dustbin fires that would normally have littered the area. All sorts of dust and debris were scattered everywhere and being churned into the stratosphere, making the going treacherous at best.

Through this infernal stormy quagmire, while all others huddled as best they could amongst their scant possessions, one man lurched uneasily along his chosen path around them. He was young, perhaps no more than twenty-five, and better dressed than all those around him. His step was unsteady, often having to balance himself against the brick of the adjacent structure. Despite the chill, he panted and sweated profusely. Something wasn't right. Now he was wheezing.

"Hey buddy, you okay?" a nearby vagrant, peering over the top of his bundled flotsam, called out.

"I...can't catch my breath, I...can't stay here..." the young man said weakly, the burgeoning gale coming close to battering him to the ground. "I don't...feel right, I..."

In an instant, he fell to his knees. He convulsed violently, his body wracked with savage seizures. His bodily functions failed him, and the sweat on his brow began to flow like a tidal wave.

"Help me...help me..." he croaked.

"Hey man!" the nearby vagrant was alarmed. "What's the matter with you?"

"I...I..."

The sweat turned into a morass of molten flesh as his face was washed away with the tide. Blood began oozing from his every pore. His facial features were now imperceptible from the rest of the mess of plasma and tissue. His entire body appeared to collapse in on itself. Within seconds there was nothing left amongst his clothes but a putrid pool of bubbling liquid.

~ Chapter 8 ~

The Wraith wrapped his cape around him like a warm, comforting blanket. While his suit was insulated somewhat against the cold, a strong northerly wind such as this was nevertheless capable of making its impact. He shivered slightly, unable to prevent his body reacting to the chilling environment.

He surveyed the city from his vantage point atop Latham Industries, high above the city streets. It was late, but despite the hour, he had recently noted Latham was still settled in his office, burning the midnight oil more ferociously than was his previous norm. That suited his purpose admirably.

Whatever it takes, I need answers from Latham.

He removed his grapnel from his belt with the aim of lowering himself down to the window of Latham's office when a cacophony of commotion from the streets below reached his ears. At such a height, it had to have been a tremendous disturbance.

What in Heaven's name?

Latham had to wait. This bore investigation.

The Wraith attached his line to the hording above and dropped swiftly and silently to an adjacent side-street. Stepping out onto Cohan Crescent, which ran perpendicular to the massive Latham Industries complex, The Wraith was met with a barrage of chaos. Many of the people milling about on the sidewalk were falling over in great distress. Cars careened into each other. Sirens roared on the air and then faded after a foul crash. Chaos. Madness.

The Wraith noted this was occurring all around him, not just on Cohan. The sounds of pandemonium reverberated throughout the city.

"Max," The Wraith spoke into his in-cowl comm-link. "We have a major emergency downtown."

"It's all over the TV," Max quickly replied. "People dropping dead all over the city without explanation."

The Wraith saw people on the street before him retching, convulsing, then collapsing in a horrific mess of bloody fluid that made even his hardened nerves flutter. Those not afflicted stood stunned and terrified by what they were witnessing.

"What could this be?" The Wraith said. "Mass poisoning? Some sort of virulent disease?" He knew Max would have no answers at this point, but asking questions was all he was currently able to do. He wasn't accustomed to feeling helpless.

"No way of knowing without further analysis," Max said in a commonsense fashion. "Get a sample quickly and bring it back to me. But be careful. I fear the worst."

Resolute, The Wraith set to work. He pulled a foldable gas mask from his belt and swiftly placed it over his face. He then sent a brief message to Sloan, who was no doubt already in-the-know, but he nevertheless informed him of the current situation. He produced a series of interconnecting vials–they resembled a series of tiny test tubes stuck together–and proceeded to collect some samples from a variety of the victims. It was stomach-churning stuff. There was little left of these poor souls.

"Help us," a bag lady cried, kneeling beside what had once been a human being, now little more than a drenched crimson bundle of clothing. She reached out to The Wraith, imploring him. His heart wept for her.

"I'm trying, ma'am," he replied, a crack in his voice. "I'll do my best to get to the bottom of this."

The lady began to cry and dropped her head in abject sorrow. The Wraith wondered if she had even heard him.

There was nothing else for it; he had to move fast. He rushed over to the alley, reached for his grapnel, and launched a line into the heavens. He was soon skyward, beginning his journey back to home base.

* * * * * *

Mayhem in Metro. People dying in the streets. Samples taken. Will update when able. Authorities need to take swift, strict action - W

No shit, Sloan thought upon reading The Wraith's message.

It was all over the news and reports were coming into police headquarters from all over the city. Some deadly affliction–perhaps a toxin, perhaps some disease–had hit Metro City like an atom bomb. Bodies reduced to puddles of...blood and gore. Casualties were already almost incalculable.

"National Guard have been called, also the CDC," Harrison said, briefing the entire department at Metro Police Plaza. "But we're needed out there as well."

"What if it's some disease?" A middle-aged cop put his hand up. "I got kids, a wife. My family..."

"We all took an oath to serve and protect," Harrison barked. "That's in good times and bad."

"But..." the middle-aged cop started.

"We have protective equipment ready and more en route with the National Guard. Should be here within the hour. Then we can get to work doing whatever we can."

Sloan nodded, looked to his partner seated beside him. She appeared concerned but trying to hide it. Fear was in her eyes. Sloan knew how she felt. In all his years on the force, he'd never seen anything like this.

And he feared this was merely the beginning.

* * * * * *

"What the hell is going on here, Kai?" Latham screamed into his cellphone.

In his office, he was glued to the television screen, watching the nightmare scenario unfold. He couldn't be sure it was Kai's fault, and yet...he just somehow knew his rogue scientist had blundered in catastrophic fashion. Either way, he had to be sure.

"I...I..." Kai said over the phone.

"What the hell happened?" Latham roared. "You were supposed to create the ultimate addictive drug, but you've unleashed some sort of horror...I don't know what...on my city!"

"It must have been the Xycosin, sir," Kai said. "Somehow it must have–"

"Xycosin!" Latham shrieked. "That poison?"

"It was supposed to bind the Ophidium molecules together. It was supposed to enhance its effect while...while...but it..."

"You madman!" Latham was beyond furious. He took a deep breath. How to settle this, how to contain this. "So...what are we dealing with here?"

There was silence on the other end of the phone for some seconds. Latham briefly wondered whether the connection was lost or...

"I cannot be certain without further investigation," Kai began, "but my surmise is that, somehow, inexplicably, the Xycosin instead of solely acting as a binding agent, has somehow caused the Ophidium to mutate into...some sort of a virus."

"Surmise?" Latham said, his annoyance building once again.

"My analysis has already begun," Kai said in a defensive tone, "but...it's early days still."

Latham groaned, gripped the bridge of his nose. Like the country–his city–needed another pandemic right now. He wasn't sure if he should even risk the trip home, such was the apparent virulence, at least according to the newscasts, of this thing. And what of a vaccine or cure?

"You better be working on an antidote or some such, Kai," Latham ordered, "or I swear, no virus will claim you before I do."

"Yes, sir, that is exactly what–"

Latham hung up.

"Dammit!" Latham said under his breath. For one of the few times in his life, he felt helpless and truly at risk of, not his liberty, but his very life.

He did not like the feeling.

* * * * * *

Both Paul, outfitted as The Wraith minus his cowl, and Max were outfitted in hazmat gear, hunched down in the Lair's lab. Max eyed a sample through a microscope, while Paul watched on as the image was projected onto a nearby screen.

"What are we looking at here, Max?"

"Well," Max said, sitting up. He pointed at the screen. "This specimen here is laced with Ophidium. See here and here?"

Paul nodded.

"But it's nothing like what we've previously encountered. It's been radically altered. Something has been added to it."

"Altered again? So quickly?"

"Oh yes," Max said. "We're clearly dealing with a master chemist, a scientist of the highest order. And I doubt many out there would be able to detect the additive as quickly as I have."

"Explain yourself."

Max stood, inched closer to the screen. "See this portion of the Ophidium cell here?"

Paul eyed it closely but, of course, it meant nothing to him without explanation.

"If I'm not mistaken, this component is Xycosin," Max said.

Paul could not suppress a gasp at hearing the name. "Xycosin."

"Indeed. We know it all too well from when Natalya Blackova launched her deadly scheme of revenge some years back."

Natalya Blackova. How ironic to hear that name again, especially since she no longer identified as that person; indeed, she had no recollection of her former life. She was now a valued member of the Global Protectors, the team of heroes he had formed to ward off the recent galactic invasion of Earth led by the monster Trigoth.

"Xycosin," Paul said again. "So, this is a case of mass poisoning, then?"

"No, I don't think so," Max said. "See this section of the cell here, and here on another sample and another, from multiple victims? The Ophidium has mutated somehow. I don't really know how. All I can do is theorize that somehow the addition of the Xycosin has caused the Ophidium to change and replicate at a fantastic rate."

"Replicate?" Paul said. He knew what that meant, dreaded the confirmation of his fears. "You mean...a virus?"

"Yes," Max said, his face darkening. "Quite possibly the deadliest virus known to mankind."

~ Chapter 9 ~

Those words were such Paul never thought he'd hear. His mind was awhirl, his thoughts jumbled. The implications for this were beyond anything he could comprehend. The entire city was at stake. Nay, the country, perhaps even the world. And what of Leena? Of Emily?

"What...what else are you able to tell me? How is this virus transmitted?" he said weakly, trying his best to pull himself together.

"Well," Max said, sounding more composed than Paul felt, "best I can tell is by respiratory droplets or airborne particles."

"Like the flu or Covid," Paul said.

"Yes, but only much more contagious, and so much more deadly. And, if my surmise is accurate, it appears to be able to survive floating in the air and on surfaces for much longer than either of those viruses." Max stopped, started rubbing his chin. "Think of it this way...if measles is super contagious in a closed room, multiply that ten-fold, maybe more, and you'll be getting closer to the mark here. And, as amazing as this may sound, being outside probably makes minimal difference."

Paul couldn't help gasping once again. This was utterly horrifying.

"Still," Max continued, rubbing his chin some more, "if the scene downtown is accurate, then there will be survivors."

"The bag lady."

"Right," Max said, snapping his fingers. "And there would likely be others. Chief, I've just had a thought. Bear with me, this will require a little probing. A few hours, perhaps. There might be a sliver of hope."

A sliver was enough.

* * * * * *

Harrison, Sloan, Perez, and other high-level detectives were congregated in Metro Police Plaza's monitor room. As the name suggested, one wall was plastered with several large monitor screens. One featured MNN's latest updates on the crisis currently unfolding, two screens featured live-cam shots of emergency personnel–police, ambulance, and fire–attempting to deal with the multitude of deaths on the city streets, another was a relay to the governor and another to the state headquarters of the CDC. It was a cacophony of chaos and abject horror.

"Commish," Sloan said, "we need to be out there. We're twiddling our thumbs here."

"You're a homicide cop, detective," Harrison said, his attention to the various screens never wavering. "We have our officers out there dealing with this as best they can until the experts arrive."

Sloan sighed but he knew Harrison was right. Still, feeling helpless was not in his ballpark. "The city's cut off from the outside world," he said as a statement rather than a question.

"Yes," Harrison replied. "All flights in and out cancelled, no road or rail traffic is permitted. The local National Guard boys, as well as our local team, are barricading every known entry into the city. No way in or out. Whatever this is that's afflicting us, we're ground zero. No reported cases have popped up anywhere else, and we want to keep it that way."

"That's a big task," Perez said. "When will the CDC personnel arrive?"

"Anytime now," Harrison replied. "The State National Guard will arrive late this afternoon to complement the local department. Lord knows we need all the help we can get."

Sloan turned his back on the screens. He'd seen enough turmoil to last him a lifetime. "Dammit, what are we dealing with here? A virus? Mass poisoning? What?"

Harrison turned and placed a reassuring hand on Sloan's shoulder. "That's what we're going to find out. I'll tell you something else..." Harrison's expression turned grim, "...if this *is* man-made, we're gonna nail whoever is responsible. Nail them!"

Sloan smiled weakly. He felt the same way, of course, but...he somehow had a feeling it wouldn't be that simple.

No, not that simple at all.

* * * * * *

Leena was at her desk in the Metro City Public Library backroom checking her work email when she heard screams, ear-shattering wails of agony, emanating from within the library.

What in Heaven's name?

She practically leaped from her chair and raced outside the staff workroom and into the public area of the library. The sight that befell her was something straight out of a Lovecraft-fueled nightmare. Near the self-checkout machines, a family–two adults, three children–were on the floor, the children screaming and weeping for their parents, who were currently in the process of melting–*melting*–before everyone watching on, helpless and in mortal terror.

Leena couldn't believe her eyes. What she was witnessing was unbearable to watch, and the smell being emanated from whatever was occurring was overpowering.

"Children," Leena cried, racing over to them and taking them in her arms.

"Mommy! Daddy!" the little girl, no more than perhaps four years old, bawled.

Leena eyed the victims. There was little left but a large, Jello-like pile of fleshy matter and blood. Lots of blood. She shielded the children's eyes, embraced them.

"It'll be okay," she said. Empty words, but it was all she could think of to say in the moment. What words could cover whatever just shattered their world?

The boy, possibly two years of age, merely sobbed silent tears. The third child, another girl, was barely two, Leena thought, and didn't really appear in tune with reality. Leena wondered if, perhaps, this girl was suffering from some sort of disability. Leena picked the two crying children up then heard further screams at another point in the library.

"Susan," Leena shouted to a library assistant manning the circulation counter, and who had previously clearly been shocked into inactivity. "Take these children out the back. Look after them. Give them some milk or something."

Without another thought, Leena raced down to the Local History section. There she saw another...body would be overstating the matter, but the clothing within the mess would indicate that was what it once was. A lady stood above it, screaming her head off.

What in the Lord's name is happening here?

She'd never seen anything like this and knew neither had The Wraith. More screams rang out, now all around her. She knew what that meant. The putrefying stench of rotting flesh now engulfed the library like the smoggy blanket that hung over Los Angeles. It was becoming all-encompassing.

She spied another assistant shelving in the aisles and beckoned her over. "Matilda, is it?" The young girl nodded. "Call 911. We have an emergency situation here. Do it now!"

Leena didn't know what else to do at present, but The Wraith had to become aware of this. She activated the emergency beacon within her Rolex Oyster Perpetual wristwatch.

If he didn't know about this already, he soon would.

* * * * * *

The light was low and dim. Azufi liked it that way. It helped to mitigate the garish pink that surrounded him, threatened to engulf him in its rank awfulness. But now, it was hardly visible. Even then, it was still too much for him. He closed his eyes.

He sighed and damned the fates once more. That seemed to be all he was capable of right now. That reality pained him even more than his current prison of pink. He tried to make sense of his situation, tried to think up a plan to...rescue him from the nightmare his life had become. He couldn't think of a thing. Not one damn thing. How was this possible? How was a captain of industry such as himself–*the* captain of industry in this town a mere moment ago–be unable to come up with a solution to his dilemma. It should be easy for someone of his caliber, his intelligence, his–

"Oh dear, why are you lying there in the dark?" Maggie-Grace said, entering the bedroom with a tray of something.

"I was about to take a nap," Azufi said bluntly.

"But it's supper time," Maggie-Grace said, unperturbed. "You can nap later, sleepy-head."

She helped–forced–Azufi to sit up, then carefully laid the tray before him. It was soup and...Azufi didn't really pay much attention to it. Maggie-Grace smiled, bent down to give Azufi a kiss, then wiped some sweat from her brow.

"My, it *is* warm in here," she said. "I'll have to check the thermostat."

Azufi gave her a look. He didn't know what the heck she was talking about. It must have been sixty-nine degrees, if anything. Barely warm, let alone hot.

"Oh my, I don't feel so well," Maggie-Grace said, starting to waver on her feet. "I feel a little...faint."

She reached up to her brow, wiped a profusion of liquid there, then lurched backward in a violent seizure.

"What the hell?" Azufi gasped.

Maggie-Grace heaved onto the bed, then fell forward, collapsing onto the tray, sending the hot soup and other contents everywhere. Azufi panicked, tried to get away, tried to unsee what was happening before him. He covered his face with his hands.

"I...I..." Maggie-Grace wheezed, then her entire body convulsed in a vicious fury. Then it was over. She was dead before Azufi even knew what had happened.

Azufi peered out from splayed fingers. He wished he hadn't, for it was at that moment Maggie-Grace, his benefactor, his lover, began to...degrade? It was almost as if her flesh was beginning to melt. Blood and goodness knew what else began to ooze then flow freely. Azufi screamed, tried to scurry from the bed, but he was in no condition for fast movement. All he managed was to flop heavily onto the floor.

Panic now built into sheer, unadulterated terror. Nothing made sense. Nothing!

He felt a drip on his forehead. The drip quickly became a torrent. He realized what it was.

He screamed.

* * * * * *

It was now night and, ordinarily, Metro City took on a whole new lease of life after the sun had set. Tonight was different. While the city lights shone bright as always, especially from such a lofty height, at street level there was nothing but bedlam. And death.

The Wraith was perched atop the Metro Mutual Insurance building. Surveying his city, listening to the various emergency broadcasts, waiting to hear from Max, wishing he could do more. But he was no doctor, no scientist. He would wait for Max, and patrol. It was then he heard the nearby explosion.

Switching on his night-vision lenses with a tap at his right temple, he narrowed his gaze in the direction of the detonation.

Where is it...wait, there.

He saw movement. He zoomed in with his lenses, saw a gang of six circling the back door of some business clearly taking advantage of the city's emergency situation of the authorities being busy elsewhere.

Scum looters.

He would show them what befell all those who would commit evil in his city.

Their time of judgment would soon be at hand.

* * * * * *

Smoke billowed from the gaping hole that had once been the service entrance to Metro City Jewelers, the most prestigious such store in downtown Metro. Rings, necklaces, wristwatches, and everything besides. Nothing stocked was below five thousand dollars, and many items were priced much, much higher than that. The six gang members, all outfitted in body-hugging black, were caught up in the maelstrom.

"You used too much explosive," one of the gang members coughed through the haze, waving his arms about frantically. "The cops will be here any second."

"No way," another gang member said. "All those dying all around us, ain't no way they have time for some...*gifting.*"

"I don't know about that," the first gang member said gruffly.

"He's right," a deep voice emanated from all around them.

"Wha...what...?" another gang member uttered.

An instant later, The Wraith was amongst them, appearing almost from nowhere, lashing out left and right.

"Your taking advantage of this city and its people is over," The Wraith grunted. "In this time of great crisis, you have been found wanting. You will thus be punished."

The Eyes of Judgment on his chest came to fiery, crackling life, its yellowish hue bathing the gang members in its ardent glare.

"To hell with that," the first gang member said, clearly itching for a fight. He would get one.

The criminal lashed out with a powerful punch, one which, had it connected, would likely have hurt The Wraith. But it was slow, uncoordinated, and The Wraith evaded it with ease.

"Whatta you guys waiting for? Let him have it," the first gang member snarled.

It took an instant, but the other gang members clearly thought it best to accede and ultimately complied. One-by-one they stepped forward, attempting to progress the attack, to surround The Wraith, forcing him on to the back foot. He was having none of it and lashed out with a spinning side kick, connecting to the jaws of four of his enemies, sending them careening to the trash-strewn alley floor.

"Arrghh," the first gang member screamed, charging at The Wraith in an attempt to catch him off guard.

The Wraith allowed his adversary to get close, then rammed his elbows down into the gang member's back. The thug dropped to the ground like a sack of cement. Before the thug had a chance to get back up, a knee to the face sent him to sleep with a bloody nose.

One thug left. The Wraith eyed him closely. The gang member appeared to tense his muscles as though about to strike, but an instant later, turned and ran, seeming to think escape the better option.

There was no escape from the Dread Avenger.

The gang member sprinted for the alley mouth, ran through it out into a narrow side street. Some bodies were strewn here and there, but it appeared otherwise deserted. He continued to run a block, then two, then made a sharp right turn into another, even darker alley. He stopped, panting ferociously, and put his hands on his knees in an attempt to catch his breath.

"You cannot escape judgment," a voice boomed from further down the alley.

The gang member gasped and the Eyes of Judgment blazed to life once more, illuminating the alley in a sickening shade of strobing yellow.

The gang member was glued to the spot, petrified. He began to shake, panting fiercely. It was all over. The Wraith latched onto the thug's head, brought it down to face the Eyes of Judgment.

"Be cleansed by a higher power," The Wraith said, "and know what it truly means to be judged."

The gang member screamed.

* * * * * *

The Wraith studied the scene around him. The looters had been taken care of, lying in a bundle, mixed with trash and effluent. One was a gibbering mess at his feet.

I better be extra vigilant tonight, The Wraith thought. *Looting in times of crisis always reaches record heights...or depths.*

His comm-link suddenly beeped an incoming message. He tapped at his left temple. "Yes, Max."

"Chief," Max said, sounding excited. "I think I've nailed something down."

"Is this what you were alluding to earlier?" The Wraith said.

"Aye," came the Irishman's eager reply. "It was just as I suspected."

"Tell me more."

"Well, you remember when we last dealt with Xycosin," Max said.

"How could I forget," he said.

"Then you'll also remember that, not too long thereafter, I came up with something that what could be termed as an antidote to that deadly poison."

"Yes, I recall," The Wraith said. "You informed us your *inoculation*, as you called it, would protect us from any future exposure to the substance."

"Aye, indeed," Max said, his excitement evidently building. "And that's been proven to be the case. But now, due to my investigation today, I can safely say with a great deal of certainty we are all immune to this Xycosin-Ophidium based virus."

"How certain?"

"As certain as I can be in such a short space of time," Max said. "But I would bet my life on it."

That was enough for The Wraith. He had learned long ago to thoroughly trust Max's instincts and intelligence. The Irishman had never let him down.

"Fine," he said. "That takes care of myself, Leena, you, and Simpson. Can you create more of this *inoculation*. This city is fast running out of time."

Max sighed into his communicator. His excitement had clearly abated. "That's where we hit a problem, Chief. I can create more of the stuff, sure, but not enough for the millions or more that need it, and certainly not fast enough to make any difference. Not with my limited capabilities here and...well...I'm just one man." He took a breath. "However, we can send the formula to Sloan, to forward onto the CDC.

They have the equipment and manpower to reproduce it at scale."

"Understood," The Wraith said. "In the meantime, how much can you make as quickly as possible?"

There was a pause. The Wraith could practically hear the cogs in Max's mind whirring. "Maybe enough for the police and emergency services. Maybe."

"Get on it, do as much as you can," The Wraith said. "And, I don't have to say it..."

"Yes, I'll hurry," Max chimed in. "I'll get Simpson down here as an extra pair of hands. That might speed things up a tad."

The Wraith nodded. "Good thinking, Max." He was about to sign off before deciding otherwise. "Oh, and Max...save a dose for Emily."

"You bet."

The Dread Avenger tapped his comm-link closed. Finally, he felt some sense of hope, some feeling they could beat this thing and ultimately save some and get the person responsible.

Until that time, he had work to do.

* * * * * *

Another all-nighter, another crisis to deal with. Latham snorted his frustration as he descended in his private elevator down to the organization's parking lot. He had decided home was the better option and decided to risk the trip there. His thoughts returned to the issue at hand. The plan had been so simple–a new, super addictive drug that would prove so potent, produce such a sense of euphoria, that those hooked would pay just about anything for another hit. A drug that would make heroin and cocaine look like a shot of lemonade. His crisis-hit empire–his kingdom–would be saved, and all would be as it was before...more-or-less.

But no, that idiot Kai couldn't deliver the goods, Latham thought. *All his promises were for naught. I'll have to deal with him. This mess has to be salvaged somehow.*

He gripped the bridge of his nose as the elevator door slid open.

"Latham, you have to help me."

"What the...?"

Latham was shocked to see Azufi, what was left of him, standing–teetering–before him. The look of fear on his erstwhile employee's face was almost comical.

"You have to help me," Azufi repeated.

"Help you? Are you mad?" Latham scoffed. The bastard was blocking his way.

"Maggie-Grace, she...she..." Azufi began to cry. Latham didn't know whether to cringe or to laugh.

"Who?" Latham said. "Get out of my way, you fool. I'm going home." He beckoned to his nearby limousine.

"But...but...you have to help me. She...died in my arms. She...she...melted..."

Latham suddenly knew what the deal was. He was repulsed. "Get away from me, you diseased clod!" He wacked Azufi with his cane and barged past.

"Hey," Azufi cried, more in desperation than bravado. "You owe me, old man. You have to help me. I don't want whatever she had...I don't want to die."

Something in Latham abruptly cracked. A fury he hadn't felt in years suddenly burst forth. He was ready to fight. To kill.

"Help–"

Azufi said not another word. Latham let fly, viciously attacking with his cane, raining blow upon blow upon the hapless Azufi's head. The former assistant was unable–incapable–of offering even a modicum of resistance, such were his previous injuries. He cried, he whimpered, he fell to the ground in the fetal position. Latham could have sworn he wept for his mommy then, ultimately, he made no sound at all.

Latham kept up his assault, each subsequent blow echoing within the parking structure. Blood splattered everywhere and bone cracked. Finally, as his cane snapped into pieces, Latham relented. He breathed heavily with the perspiration to match, but he somehow also felt exhilarated. He hadn't let loose with such violence personally since he had been a much younger man. He relished the memory. He couldn't help but smile. Azufi lay at his feet in a horrendous mix of blood and bone.

Latham brushed down his impeccable, albeit blood-spattered, Italian tailored suit, rubbed his hands together. The job was done. He turned and almost bumped into his chauffeur standing there behind him.

"Did you enjoy the show?" Latham said after a brief pause.

"Yes, sir," the chauffeur replied, not all together convincingly.

Latham smirked. He didn't care what his driver thought. "Take me home."

"Do you need help to the car? Your cane," the driver said, offering his boss a hand. Latham smacked it aside.

"I can make my own way. Just take me home."

The chauffeur nodded and spun on his heels, reaching the driver's seat in but a few moments. He kept his vision away from Latham, the crime lord noted, as Latham shuffled forward slowly until he ultimately reached the rear seat.

"Drive," Latham ordered sharply.

The chauffeur gunned the vehicle to life, began to edge toward the exit, when Latham suddenly said, "No, over there." He pointed at Azufi's prone body. "Let's make sure of the job."

"Yes...sir," the chauffeur said.

The driver aimed the limousine at Azufi's body and promptly ran it over with an audible bump.

"Shall I...?" the chauffeur started.

"Again?" Latham pondered the question briefly. "No, Smithers, I think that arriviste has had enough. If he lives, which I doubt, he deserves whatever befalls him. Now...take me home."

They had barely exited the parking lot when Latham's cell rang. "Yes?" A pause. "Kai. What's this? You say you have an antidote? I'll be right there." He took a deep breath. Perhaps Kai will live to see another day after all. "Smithers, take me to the lab."

~ Chapter 10 ~

Sloan barged out from the monitor room. He had seen enough to know Metro City was on the cusp of annihilation. To his mind it wasn't negativity, or a loss of hope, just unequivocal realism. He'd always been a straight shooter.

"Sloan, wait," Perez cried after him.

"For what?" Sloan said, continuing down the hallway toward their desks. "I'm done feeling helpless. At least I can get through some paperwork while society is collapsing all around us. At least that's *something*."

"That's not like you," Perez said, drawing alongside her partner. "You're not suffering from that–"

"No, Perez, I'm fine, I promise you," Sloan said. "I just see the writing on the wall, is all. Nothing more."

He looked to his partner, saw her expression of bewilderment–of sadness, even–but shrugged it off. She'll come to see his point of view in the end, he felt.

As they approached their desks, Sloan saw a non-descript package leaning up against his computer. It was blank save for a small yellow image of what he knew to be a depiction of the Eyes of Judgment. It was something from The Wraith himself. He opened it eagerly.

"Mail call?" Perez said, an eyebrow raised.

He ignored her, scanned the interior contents. There was a sheaf of papers featuring some gibberish he couldn't make hide nor hair of as well as a short note, which read:

This is the formula and instructions for an antidote and vaccine to the current plague. Send it to the CDC immediately for replication and wide distribution. Make this your immediate *priority - W.*

Sloan's eyes bulged open. He couldn't believe what he was reading but, as he thought more about it, why should he be surprised? This was The Wraith, after all, capable of virtually any amazing feat and, in truth, when had he ever let the people of Metro down?

"What is it?" Perez said. She had no doubt noted Sloan's bewildered expression.

"Hope," Sloan replied. "Salvation." He stood quickly, brandishing the package and its contents.

"Huh?" she said and stood as well. "Where are you going?"

"Wait right there," he said sharply. "I have to deliver this package."

He rushed away.

* * * * * *

Latham shuffled as best he could into the secret laboratory he had set up for Daniel Kai. The scientist sat stolidly at his desk up ahead, as though he hadn't a care in the world. Latham wasn't exactly sure what the ultimate outcome of this meeting would be. He was making no promises to anyone, least of all himself.

"What have you got, Kai?" he asked as he reached the scientist's desk.

Kai swiveled in his chair. "Mr. Latham, sir. I have here the answer to our problem." He held aloft a syringe.

"Your problem, Kai. *Your* problem," Latham said.

"Yes, well..." Kai said, his face clouding over.

"All right, let's hear your spiel. What have you got there?"

"Ah..." Kai said, brightening up. "Well, I *was* able to ascertain that the Ophidium-Xycosin mix did, indeed, evolve into a most virulent virus."

"Yes, yes, I know all this," Latham said, impatient. "Though I have noticed some appear to be already immune. I, for one, have not succumbed."

"Natural selection," Kai said with a sniff. "Throughout history there have always been some who proved immune to even the deadliest of plagues. Or our species would have become extinct long ago."

"Harrumph," Latham snorted with some derision.

"Well, here is a cure, if you will, for this virus," Kai said, apparently ignoring Latham's attitude, raising the syringe in the air once again.

"A cure?" Latham was skeptical.

"Yes, well, vaccine would be a more appropriate appellation. Once injected, the subject will become completely immune to the virus."

Latham took a moment to take it all in. He knew Kai was a genius in microbiology and recombinant DNA, but...well, he had failed in his primary function up to this point.

"How certain are you of this?" Latham said, his eyes tightening.

Kai appeared offended at that statement. "I am an intellectual giant in my field, if I may say. None could have achieved what I have done in such record time. I would not rely on natural selection to spare you."

"Fine," Latham said, wanting to shut down the conversation. "Fine."

"I have already fully tested the vaccine," Kai continued, clearly agitated, "on everyone in this laboratory, including myself. *That* is how I am certain of my findings."

Latham nodded, raised both eyebrows. He was impressed, though not with Kai's rampaging arrogance, even if it was partially deserved.

"Your arm please, sir," Kai said, pointing to Latham's right arm.

Latham acquiesced, removing his suit coat and rolling up his shirt sleeve. "Get it over with then."

Kai administered the shot with a smile. He must have felt some satisfaction at, no doubt to his mind, his winning the argument. Latham left well enough alone.

"How much more of this do you have?" Latham said.

"What do you mean?"

"My organization, my employees, need this protection. My company cannot function without them, and I certainly can't hire thousands of new staff all at once, if there is anyone left after all this," Latham said.

"Yes, I see," Kai said, somewhat vacantly. "I shall endeavor to have enough samples of the vaccine at your disposal."

"Make it fast while I still have some staff left," Latham said. "An intellectual giant in your field can surely achieve that."

His dig at Kai did not go unnoticed, Latham could tell, but Kai held his emotions in check. "Very well, sir. I shall work around the clock to have it ready for you."

Latham smiled. Now it was his turn to feel some satisfaction. "Splendid. Arrange for delivery and the administering of the medication at my office as quickly as possible. I want this settled...now!"

He put his jacket back on and retreated. Mid-stride, he stopped suddenly and whirled to face Kai. "And if another, better drug isn't created by the end of the month...you won't live to see the following one." He'd had enough of this arrogant prick. Kai had served a purpose today, yes, but he'd ultimately failed in his primary mission, and Latham was doubtful that could be rectified in any way. But he'd give him one last chance, otherwise he would rectify it himself.

* * * * * *

The Wraith continued his patrol. Apart from a bunch of looters, which was proving a serious problem that night, he had also dealt with a major drug deal gone wrong, two attempted rapes, and one attempted kidnapping. And, relatively speaking, the night was still young. He dreaded the further conflicts he would likely face. This plague had certainly brought out the city's crazies, he thought.

"I decided you could use some help," a familiar voice rang out from behind him.

The Wraith couldn't help but smile and turned to face Leena outfitted as Lady Wraith. "I definitely could. It's been hectic to say the least."

"Max has filled me in on the latest developments," she said. "I hope the CDC can move fast on this."

"Yes," The Wraith agreed. "Lives are at stake. Millions of lives."

"The government has to step in with the fullest resources they have available," she said.

"No doubt they will. Even so, it will take time. All we can do is hold the line until then."

"Where to next, then?" she said.

"Well..." he started.

He stopped at the sudden commotion coming from the street below. Both of them peered over the edge of the building, witnessed a high-stakes, high speed car chase taking place beneath them. The raucous siren of a police cruiser floated up at them.

"We're needed," The Wraith said.

"Lead on."

* * * * * *

"I need backup," the harried cop cried into his radio. "Perp is heading south on Tenth Street in a stolen Camero, license plate FZK 8327. He doesn't seem to care what damage he causes en route. I'm staying in pursuit but need backup to end this quickly."

"Roger that," came a voice over the radio. "We're a little short right now, but we'll try and get you some assistance when we can. Out."

The cop grunted, then swerved the car violently to the right to avoid an abandoned car in the middle of the road. He frantically gripped the wheel, tried his best to maintain pursuit of his quarry, but to no avail. Braking, his cruiser skidded into an adjacent traffic light. The chase was over.

The cop took a few moments to catch his breath, then realized his airbag hadn't deployed. Thankfully his seat belt had held firm.

"Freakin' airbag!"

"Are you okay?" a female voice suddenly sounded beside him.

"Wha..." the cop said, startled. He turned to see Lady Wraith positioned in the passenger seat.

"I didn't mean to startle you," she said.

"L...Lady Wraith?" the cop said, a little unsure of himself.

She smiled. "You appear uninjured."

He nodded.

"Good. This city needs all the help it can get."

"I...I was pursuing a perp..." he started.

"Yes, we know," she said softly.

"W...we?"

Lady Wraith smiled again. "Your quarry won't get far."

* * * * * *

"Ha! Damn cop," the carjacker said with a smirk. "Got what he deserved."

The carjacker sped away fast. One look in his rearview mirror and the police cruiser was already disappearing from sight. In moments he'd be free and clear.

Abruptly, his view through the windshield became completely obscured.

"What the f...!"

He gripped the wheel tighter, began to swerve left and right in an attempt to shake the...whatever it was free. Some sort of canvas, or blanket or...

In a blur of movement, the windshield cleared and was instantly replaced with a strange, whizzing sound. It seemed to come from above, or around, or maybe...in front of him?

His foot was still on the gas when he finally spotted it–a small, circular disc on the windshield off to the right. And...there was a flashing light on it.

"What the–?"

Seconds later, he was showered with a flood of shattered glass, the entire windshield exploding in a violent fashion.

Caught off guard, he struggled with the wheel, vainly trying to maintain control. Before he could do anything else, an arm reached through the open windshield, grabbed him by the shirt collar, and yanked him out and up onto the roof.

"Yaaahhhh!"

The carjacker had no time to ascertain who had him or what had really occurred. It was all so swift, so fierce, so...

"Judgment is coming for you," a voice spoke. Seconds later they were both careening through the air. As they landed heavily on the sidewalk, the carjacker grunted in pain, then heard an almighty crash. He swiveled to witness his car going up in flames further down the boulevard.

"What...what just happened?" he said, trying to pump the air back into his lungs. He gripped his shoulder. It stung and he grimaced trying to move it.

"Your morals have been found wanting–"

The carjacker finally had the wherewithal to comprehend the situation he now found himself in. He was standing before The Wraith.

"–and judgment will thusly be administered."

The carjacker's mouth was agape, or so he felt. Never had he thought he would ever see, let alone meet, the mythical Dread Avenger of the Underworld. And here he was, now facing the vigilante every punk in the city–and beyond–feared. His muscles tensed then began to vibrate ever-so-slightly. Those vibrations quickly morphed into stronger tremors, tremors of fright, and he realized this could very well be his end.

* * * * * *

The Wraith loomed large, could see his target was beginning to falter, to fear the judgment that would soon be upon him. He had reason to fear.

"You will face the pain you have inflicted on others," The Wraith said. "You will feel it and deal with it. Judgment is here!"

He stepped forth, about to administer the Judgment Stare, when something caught his eye further down the street. There was movement and it–*he*–was large. An instant to check–could that be...?

An instant was all it took. While he was distracted, the carjacker reclaimed his nerve and tossed a handful of dirt and pebbles from the gutter into The Wraith's face. He darted off like a jackrabbit.

The Wraith took a few moments to clear his vision, just in time to see his prey on the lam down the street. The person he had briefly seen was now nowhere in sight. A mystery he had no time to dwell on.

A cold wind had picked up, causing trash and grit to flow freely through the air. A burst of lightning showered the street in a brief but wondrous flash, followed by a mighty thunderclap. A storm was brewing and, from the sounds of it, edging closer. Sprinting in pursuit, The Wraith caught sight of the carjacker turning left up ahead into Mooney Avenue as the heaven's opened, making the going ever more treacherous.

He quickly followed, but the miscreant had a good head start on him. Traffic was non-existent due to the existential crisis Metro currently found itself in, but the rain made the streets slippery, moreso with the remains of the city's dead mixed in amongst it. The city was largely deserted save for a plethora of bodies reduced to roiling puddles all around him. The thought of what had happened to these people, the turmoil gripping his city, turned The Wraith's stomach.

Mind on the job, man. Mind on the job.

He was gaining on his quarry. The carjacker started to falter, kept turning back to check if his pursuer was still following. The Wraith pressed on, vaulting bodies and rounding empty vehicles. His stamina knew no bounds when he was on the hunt.

The rain quickly turned into a torrential downpour as the carjacker ducked into a narrow alley off Mooney. The Wraith couldn't help but smile. He knew that alley led nowhere. Now, the thief would be his.

Entering the alley cautiously, The Wraith edged forward, slow and but steady. Even with the cacophony of the building storm, he could have sworn he heard a scrambling up ahead. Another flash of lightning and he caught sight of his prey. The carjacker had reached the end of the road and was scratching and tearing for some way out. Or up. There was no escape.

"There is no evading judgment," The Wraith said, continuing his advance. "You must atone for your sins."

The carjacker whirled, came face-to-face once again with his pursuer. He initially appeared panic-stricken, then his demeanor changed somewhat. Perhaps realizing his only way out was to fight. As such, the carjacker assumed a fighting stance. And the battle, such as it was, commenced.

The carjacker thought the best defense was offense and lunged at the Dread Avenger with various punches. None connected. He wasn't unskilled exactly, but no doubt due to the rain and the stress of the situation, he lacked coordination. Either way, he was no match for The Wraith.

"End this charade," The Wraith said. "Judgment will not wait."

The Wraith evaded another blow and another. And yet another. The carjacker was starting to waver, his strength and stamina swiftly fading. The Wraith lashed out with a straight right to the face. The carjacker fell flat on his rear.

"The time for judgment is now!" The Wraith said, yanking the hapless thief to his feet and drawing his head into position to administer the Judgment Stare.

"That pitiful creature is beneath you," a voice beckoned from The Wraith's rear.

The Wraith swirled, dropping the carjacker onto the wet asphalt. It was pitch dark until another bolt from the heavens illuminated the alley. The Wraith was shocked to see Blackstorm standing at the far end of the lane. His appearance was as the others both he and Lady Wraith had recently faced. Formidable foes, apparent lackeys of none other than the Cobra himself.

Blackstorm? Another one? How is this possible?

"You need to answer for your recent transgressions," Blackstorm said, his voice as deep as it was harsh.

"Who are you working for?" The Wraith said above the din of the storm. "The Cobra? Where is he?"

"You dare not speak his name," Blackstorm said. "You are not fit to even sight his shadow."

"Your gibbering is useless to me," The Wraith said. "You will give me the answers I seek."

"Then come get them," Blackstorm said, beckoning The Wraith to come forward. "If you can."

The Wraith gritted his teeth.

~ Chapter 11 ~

Sloan sauntered into the central squad room at Metro Police Plaza and plonked down at his desk. He was satisfied. Perez, going over some case notes at her desk opposite, eyed him with a suspicious glance, he noted.

"Where have you been?" she asked. "What was that package all about?"

"This city's salvation," he said.

"What? C'mon, don't hide anything from me."

"I'm not," Sloan said, still not entirely telling the truth. He leaned over his desk closer to Perez, spoke in hushed tones. "I mean, I don't mean to. That package came from The Wraith. A cure for the pandemic." Her eyes bulged wide open. She moved to speak, but Sloan held his hands up. She held her tongue. "I have a contact at the CDC, an old marine buddy. I passed the details on to him."

"So, wait...what? A cure? How can you trust this is legit? Where did this package come from...oh wait...The Wraith."

He winked at her. At least she now understood. Or at least Sloan hoped she would.

"I don't get it, Bob," Perez said. "You and The Wraith are now bosom buddies?"

"We have an...understanding. Let's leave it at that."

Perez rolled her eyes and sighed. Sloan knew that would be the end of it. His partner wouldn't take it any further...at least for the time being.

"Okay then, what does this all mean? CDC?"

"They now have the formula for a vaccine to inoculate the population," he explained.

"That'll take time. It's a big job," she said.

"You're right. But it's a start, and they're the only ones capable of pulling it off."

Sloan carefully removed some ampules from his coat pocket.

"What have you got there?" Perez said.

"The vaccine...for us, most of us here in the building," Sloan said. "You gonna help me explain this to Harrison?"

Perez's eyes narrowed. He knew what she was thinking. He didn't envy what would come next either.

* * * * * *

A tremendous clap of thunder and the fight began in earnest. The Wraith thought it best to go on the immediate offensive, lashing out with powerful lefts and rights and spinning kicks. It was like attacking a brick wall. Blackstorm was already large and powerful, but he was also at least partially armored, which made any onslaught all the more difficult.

"Is this the best you can do?" Blackstorm mocked. "How you defeated the others, why my master considers you a threat, I cannot comprehend."

The Wraith knew Blackstorm was trying to distract him, enrage him, make him sloppy. It would not work. "You will reveal all to me, and you will face just judgment." The Eyes of Judgment burst into fervent life.

"Your parlor tricks do not concern me," Blackstorm said. "I will prove to my master I am his rightful heir...and you are but nothing to him. Or me."

"Chief," Max's voice came over The Wraith's comm-link.

"Not now, Max," The Wraith barked.

"Riots downtown," Max said, ignoring his boss. "Survivors rioting, not enough emergency personnel to control them. Heading your way."

The Wraith filed the knowledge away. He had other things to deal with at present. Blackstorm pressed forward this time. The Wraith didn't wait, launching another attack of his own. This time he lobbed a smoke pellet at Blackstorm's feet, enveloping the villain in a thick, acrid haze. In the villain's confusion, The Wraith landed blow after blow. Even with Blackstorm's size and armor in his favor, The Wraith knew he was beginning to hurt his opponent. A knee to the solar plexus, an uppercut to the jaw, and Blackstorm was set back on his haunches. As the smoke cleared, it was obvious Blackstorm was hurting.

"You...will not...best me," Blackstorm grunted.

Then, moving faster than anyone that size had any right to, Blackstorm charged at The Wraith, taking the Dread Avenger off guard, and lifting the hero up in a mighty bear hug.

"Arrgghh," The Wraith muttered.

He tried valiantly to extricate himself from his adversary's clutches, but he could find no purchase, his gloves slipping off Blackstorm's drenched clothing. A second later, he felt sure a rib had snapped. Blackness was looming, then death.

No, not now. Not like this.

An instant more, and The Wraith found himself on his knees, free and violently coughing in a desperate attempt to fill his lungs with air. His vision blurred briefly, but he could have sworn he saw Blackstorm lying face down in a substantial puddle on the alley floor. What had happened?

"Your evil will not triumph this day," a familiar voice said.

The Wraith smiled. It was Lady Wraith, who had tracked him down in the nick of time. He was in pain, a suspected cracked rib, but nothing more. And, with his lungs replenished and Lady Wraith joining him, a renewed strength filled his limbs.

He was ready for round two.

Blackstorm's legs were pinned by Lady Wraith's grapnel line. It was virtually unbreakable. The Wraith stepped forward, reached down, and yanked the villain up to his knees. He let fly with powerful blows to the face. Left and right, one after the other in quick succession. He did not wish Blackstorm any time to recover, to regain composure. Again and again The Wraith connected, sending the villain's head snapping to and fro.

"You will reveal all you know," The Wraith said, never letting up the barrage of violence. "And you will never sully this city with your presence again. Judgment will be administered."

In one last, swift movement, The Wraith swiped the villain's mask from him, revealing a non-descript young man of perhaps Middle Eastern appearance. The Eyes of Judgment burst into life once more.

"I will never betray my master," Blackstorm said, spitting in The Wraith's face as he did so. "I would rather die than live with this dishonor. Being bested by such...inferior infidels."

The Wraith heard a cracking sound emanating from Blackstorm's mouth and the villain collapsed, falling in a soggy heap, limp as a wet sock. It was over.

"Same as the others we've met in recent times," Lady Wraith said, now standing by The Wraith's side. "Taken his own life rather than live with the shame of defeat."

"What puts that sort of fear into a man?" The Wraith said, reaching up to his injured side.

"Not what. Who."

The Wraith knew the implications of that. Indeed, he feared it. Feared for the fate of the city and its people.

"You're hurt," Lady Wraith said, obviously noticing The Wraith's pained expression.

"A rib," he said. "I'll be fine."

"I'll be the judge of that," she said firmly. "We're heading for home base."

Before The Wraith could respond, they were interrupted by the raucous disturbance that was clearly a large crowd of angry people heading their way.

"What the...?" Lady Wraith began.

"A riot," The Wraith broke in. "Max informed me of it moments ago."

Lady Wraith appeared troubled. "What can we do?"

The Wraith didn't immediately answer. In truth, he had no immediate answer to give. Then, he raced to the end of the alley, peered out into Mooney. Further down the street, a wave of people marched forward, screaming, throwing trash and brandishing what appeared to be trash can lids, baseball bats, and broken bottles.

"How many?" she said, standing behind the Dread Avenger and unable to see for herself the carnage on its way.

"Too many."

The Wraith, thinking quickly, searched around him, spotted a nearby abandoned car with the driver's side door open.

"Quickly," he said, indicating to the empty Buick.

Lady Wraith did not hesitate, bounded over to it and jumped into the passenger side. The Wraith was instantly beside her, hot-wiring the car into life. With a hot slip of rubber, The Wraith launched the vehicle forward, toward the battalion of angry men and women heading straight for them.

"There's so many of them," Lady Wraith said.

The Wraith clenched his jaw. He didn't know how this would pan out but he had to try something. Who knew where these rioters would ultimately end up, or what they would ultimately do to others as well as themselves. They were mad, distraught, not thinking clearly.

Lost.

The Buick careened down Mooney, the swarm of people not hesitating in their continued, violent march. As they neared, The Wraith yanked at the wheel, turning the car sideways as it skidded to a sudden halt. The Wraith leaped out and up onto the roof of the car.

"People of Metro," he cried at the top of his lungs. "Stop your march. Salvation will soon be yours." He spread his cloak outward, the breeze catching it, casting an ominous shadow outward.

Lady Wraith joined him, held up her hands at the milling masses. "Please, listen!"

"The city authorities will be distributing a cure for the pandemic shortly," The Wraith shouted, but it made little difference above the building din. The crowd either didn't hear him or didn't care.

They had nearly reached their car when another car slid to a halt alongside them. The Wraith turned first, saw it was the cop that had previously been chasing the carjacker. He'd gotten his beat-up sedan going again and had joined them in their futile cause.

The cop exited his car quickly, brandishing a pump-action shotgun and fired one round into the air. That halted the rioters at once. The cop jumped up onto the Buick and stood alongside the two heroes. He pointed his gun out into the crowd.

"Enough," the cop shouted. "I have an entire squadron on its way here, fully armed. Lay down your weapons and return to your homes and families."

"My family is gone," one man near the front of the crowd cried out in anguish. "They're dead. I have nothing left."

"Nobody is helping us," another added, "we've been left to fend for ourselves. No advice, no solutions. We've heard nothing."

Others yelled out similar such stories of anguish and helplessness. The Wraith caught Lady Wraith shedding a tear out of the corner of his eye.

"I give you my word," The Wraith said, "that help is on the way. My team has arranged a vaccination that will be given to every citizen of this city."

The cacophony of shouting now gave way to a murmuring, a mix of hope and, perhaps, a little confusion.

The cop, stiff as a board, kept his shotgun trained on the crowd.

"Who the hell are you?" another man in the crowd spat.

"You know who I am," The Wraith said. "And I will always do all I can to keep you all safe."

The unintelligible murmuring now turned to soft chanting of The Wraith's name. They knew him and they knew he spoke the truth. They were coming round.

"Listen to the man," the cop yelled, his aim never wavering. "Leave the streets, return to your homes now."

The Wraith held up his hands in unison with Lady Wraith. He didn't want to lose the power of the moment.

"Please," he said, "I speak the truth. Return home and you will be safe."

Two men at the head of the group of rioters dropped their makeshift weapons. Another followed, then another and another. Finally, everyone lost their appetite for mayhem and gave up the fight. Slowly they turned and began the steady march back from whence they came.

The three watched the crowd intently as they ultimately disappeared into a side-street far down Mooney. At last, The Wraith felt like he could breathe again. He turned to Lady Wraith to his right.

"Thanks heavens," he said, taking another deep breath.

"We did it," Lady Wraith said, visibly shaken.

"Hey," the cop said, only now lowering his weapon, "is what you said true? There's some kind of cure coming?"

"There is," The Wraith said. "Your department should be informing you of this shortly."

The cop seemed to relax somewhat upon hearing this. "Hey man, I can't thank you enough."

"No, thank you," Lady Wraith said.

The Wraith knew what she meant. It was this police officer's timely arrival that, truly, saved the day, halting the rioter's momentum and thusly allowing The Wraith to convince them of his words.

"Well," the cop said, wiping the sweat from his brow, "I don't know what else to say."

"There's no need," The Wraith said.

He motioned to Lady Wraith, who instantly understood him. They both reached to their belts, produced their grapnel guns, and fired their lines skyward. An instant more and the cop was fast receding into the distance.

* * * * * *

"Has everyone here been inoculated?" Commissioner Harrison bellowed into the squad room. "Give me a show of hands."

Everyone raised a hand, including Sloan and Perez.

"All right, you're all cleared for external duties. Get out there and help."

Harrison retreated down the hallway toward his own office. Perez looked at her partner across their desks. "I'm surprised how well he took it."

Sloan shrugged. "I think he's secretly a fan of The Wraith."

"A fan?"

"Well, maybe fan's not the right word for it," he said, standing, "but he's never said a word against The Wraith, has he? He's never issued an edict to apprehend him. Think about it."

"I guess..." Perez said, also standing. "But..."

"It doesn't matter," he said, pulling his jacket from the back of his chair. "We've been given the all-clear. Let's get back to work. The boys out there could use a helping hand."

Perez nodded and followed him out towards the exit. "But what about the CDC? Any word from your contact?"

"They're replicating the vaccine as a matter of top priority," Sloan explained while walking, "but it'll still take some time to create the stuff in large enough quantities." He barged out the station's front door, down the stairs toward the sidewalk, Perez in tow. It felt good to get out into the fresh air, or what passed as fresh air in Metro.

"What does that mean exactly? How long? Any estimate?"

"He couldn't be precise," Sloan said. "Maybe two weeks until they *begin*. I stress the word 'begin' to vaccinate survivors. Could well be a month."

Perez started to react then nodded slowly, perhaps realizing the enormity of the task at hand. He understood her concern. At least he no longer felt quite as helpless as he had earlier, but now a different emotion was welling within him, a much more damaging emotion.

Guilt. Survivor's guilt.

Perez must have noticed a change within him. "You okay, Bob?"

He shrugged the feeling off. "I'll be fine. Now, let's get out there. You heard Harrison: let's try and help some people."

They made their way to their unmarked, but one more thing gnawed at Sloan. Vaccinating the people was all well and good but...

He just hoped there would be enough people left alive to vaccinate.

* * * * * *

The door to the lab blasted open, revealing a battalion of armed guards. All were outfitted in black-ops paraphernalia, brandishing machine guns. They swarmed through the secret laboratory, one by one letting out a cry of all-clear.

After the final such cry, Robert Latham shuffled in and was stunned by the sight that befell him. The lab was empty, completely cleaned out of equipment and personnel. Nothing remained and, more importantly, there was no sign of Daniel Kai.

"Sonuva..." Latham said under his breath. "The nerd has betrayed me."

Of course, Latham had come to terminate the scientist that had so gravely failed him despite apparently giving Kai a chance to redeem himself at their last meeting, but that was neither here nor there. In truth, he had no intention of giving him another chance. There would be no second chances in his newly-built kingdom. Latham grunted. The betrayal, the fact Kai had the wherewithal–the *balls*–to up and take everything like this...Latham didn't know whether to be impressed or chagrined. The latter emotion won out. And he was mad.

"We've checked every room, sir," an armed guard said, coming up to Latham. "There's no sign of any life."

Latham grunted again. Then, he spotted something on the far wall, something...white? "What's that?"

The armed guard before Latham turned and looked in that direction. He loped down the vast, warehouse-sized room, grabbed at the wall, then quickly returned.

"It's a note, sir," the guard said.

"I can see that," Latham said, snatching at the note. It read:

Mr. Latham. I thought it the better part of valor to retreat. I have sadly realized that, despite my expertise, a drug with the qualities you desire is not something I can create in the timeframe given. I know that is not the answer you wish to acknowledge. I also know you will wish to seek retribution against me, to try and hunt me down for failing you. As such, I will never be safe unless I take the course of action I have chosen. Good luck and God speed - D. Kai.

A deeper fury began to well inside him. The utter...

"Hey, what's that ticking?" another guard said further down the way.

"What was that?" Latham said, not sure if he had heard correctly. "Ticking?" Latham's eyes opened wide at the sudden realization. "Get out, everyone get out! A bomb!"

Latham was as close to panic as he ever cared to be. He knew he was in no condition to make a run for it. He was closer to the exit than anyone else, but with all the guards barging past him, there was no way he was getting out in quick time. He was done for.

Damn you, Kai.

Latham closed his eyes, preparing for the end, when powerful arms encircled him, actually lifting him off the floor and careening him out toward the exit. In what seemed a blur of movement, he was being yanked up the fire stairs and up and out of the building. It wasn't until he was out on the sidewalk and crossing the street that he realized the guard who had brought him the note was carrying him to safety. It was pouring with rain.

In moments, they had reached the opposite side of the street and had ducked into an alley when the brownstone they had only moments ago been deep inside erupted in a massive conflagration of concrete and steel. The detonation was as mighty as anything Latham had ever seen or heard. Even around the corner of the adjacent building, Latham could have sworn he felt the heat of the inferno upon the skin of his sodden face.

"Holy geez!" Latham uttered as he and his rescuer slowly rounded the corner, catching sight of the blazing holocaust across the street. The brownstone was largely gone, save for the very lowest portion, replaced by flames and debris raining down all around them.

"It's not safe here, sir," the guard said. There was no sight of any of the other guards around. "I need to get you to a place of refuge."

"Yes," Latham agreed. "By all means."

"This way, sir," the guard motioned back into the alley.

Latham edged down into the shadows, with the light from the nearby blaze flickering on the surrounding walls around them, casting the scene into an eerie, Hellish landscape.

After a few moments, Latham came to a stop.

"We really should be–" the guard said.

"What's your name, son?"

"John," the guard said. "John Carruthers."

"Carruthers," Latham announced, "you saved my life. My organization could use a man like you. *I* could use a man like you. Interested?"

"Yes, sir," John Carruthers replied eagerly.

"Good," Latham said, a smile on his face. "Come, let us be away from here."

The two quickly disappeared into the darkness of the Metro night.

* * * * * *

"What was that?" Lady Wraith said, turning suddenly.

The two of them were currently situated on an office roof. They had been there to catch their breaths before heading for home, until...

"An explosion," The Wraith replied. "Not too far from here by the sounds of it."

"There," Lady Wraith said, pointing toward the north side of the city.

A cloud of flame and smoke was erupting almost from within the very depths of the city. From their distance, The Wraith couldn't make out the exact source of the blast, but it was likely some sort of building, possibly residential, judging from the inferno's location.

"We should investigate," Lady Wraith said.

Before The Wraith could answer, a ruckus began to build in the streets beneath them. Larger, louder than before.

"Another riot," Lady Wraith said, peering down at the sight of the commotion. "This time twice the size."

The Wraith grunted, both in pain and frustration. Would their struggles never end this night? "We need some serious backup."

"I'll let Sloan know," she said, activating her in-cowl comm-link. "We need the riot squad here fast!"

The Wraith's mind was abuzz with options—or the lack of them. Until help arrived, a frenetic crowd of this size was beyond their ability to stop, let alone control. Even stun pellets wouldn't be enough to knock them all out, nor smoke pellets enough to distract them to enable the two of them to take them all out. It was too much, it was all just too much.

"Sloan says they'd already dispatched the squad a few minutes ago. Should be on-site shortly," Lady Wraith reported.

The Wraith rallied at that. Hope was restored. He took a few deep breaths. Painful as it was, due to his injuries, it also helped to clear his mind and re-focus his energies to the impending task.

"They're heading down Seventh," she said, "smashing cars and business fronts as they go."

"I hope Sloan and his team arrive quickly," he said, "or there won't be much of a city left to save."

"Look!" Lady Wraith shouted, pointing a far distance down Seventh.

The Wraith activated his in-cowl telescopic lenses. Barricades were already being set up by what appeared to be the National Guard. The barricades were thin, the Guard sparse. The Wraith wasn't sure they could hold their ground.

"They won't hold back this swarm," The Wraith said, switching his lenses off. "We have to head down there, do whatever we can to help until the big guns arrive."

Lady Wraith nodded her head solemnly. "Lead the way."

* * * * * *

A battalion of angry people barreled forward down what had once been a bustling, fashionable boulevard, screaming, chanting, bashing violently at anything around them.

The Wraith and Lady Wraith landed atop an armored vehicle, startling several of the National Guardsmen. The remainder of the barricades were regular sedans no doubt purloined from what was readily available in the street.

"Captain," The Wraith said to the one he noted was in charge of the ten guardsmen in situ. "These barricades aren't enough."

"I know it," the captain shouted above the din, "but this is all we could wrangle in such quick time. We're spread pretty thin."

"Reinforcements are on the way," Lady Wraith said, breathing heavily.

"Maybe," the captain said, "but there are other riots scattered throughout the city."

"We dealt with one already," The Wraith said.

"Okay," the captain said, clearly perturbed. "Who the hell are you people and how do you know so much about our operations?"

"No time to explain," The Wraith said. "Here they come!"

The army of rioters were almost upon them. The guardsmen raised their weapons, the captain fired skyward.

"Halt!" the captain shouted into a megaphone. "Return to your homes!"

They either couldn't hear him or didn't care, for they continued their inexorable march, violent intent writ large on their faces. They were baying for blood.

"I don't want to fire on them," the captain said, clearly becoming alarmed. "But I will if I have to."

"There's too many," The Wraith said, "and you'll just enrage the survivors even more."

They were just a few feet away now.

"Then what do we do?" The captain started to sound a little frantic.

"Whatever we can," The Wraith said as he leaped down from his position to the street below.

Lady Wraith gasped but followed suit.

"Quickly," The Wraith said, "throw as many smoke pellets into the crowd as you have. We need to distract them."

Lady Wraith instantly did as requested and The Wraith did likewise. Pellet after pellet landed at the feet of the oncoming horde, an acrid smoke exploding upward into their faces. Utter confusion reigned supreme, and The Wraith needed to take swift advantage of that. With a battle cry like an ancient, barbaric warrior, he entered the fray as a man possessed, lashing out with all his might with blow after mighty blow. As the rioters flayed about, blinded and baffled, the two heroes battled valiantly, trying to subdue as many of the crowd as humanly possible before the vapor cleared. The Wraith hoped that by taking as many out as they could, the rest would think better of the endeavor.

He hoped.

Lady Wraith joined the fight, and both mowed through their adversaries rapidly and efficiently. Body after body fell at their feet and, with the smoke starting to clear, they dared not tarry for an instant. They pressed on with their attack, kicking and punching with everything they had.

The Wraith allowed himself a fleeting moment to glance upward. He wished he hadn't. Onward and onward they kept coming, and now their vision was restored. It would be only moments before they were overcome, and all might still be lost.

The Wraith's reverie was broken by the explosive sound of automatic gunfire behind him. Everything stopped for a moment.

"My men and I will fire on you if you force our hand," the captain shouted, "make no mistake of that. If you persist you will be taken down."

The Wraith then realized the captain had fired his rounds into the air. His gambit had worked, the rioters were frozen to the spot, not sure whether it was worth it to continue, no doubt measuring whether the captain truly meant what he said. Apprehension, and anger, filled the very air around them.

"You won't fire on innocent civilians," one burly man yelled in defiance, waving his fist in the air. "You're sworn to protect and defend."

"Guess again." The captain aimed his gun at the man and fired at his feet, apparently nicking a toe in the process.

"Hey!" the burly man cried out. "You shot me!"

The captain and his men raised their weapons and aimed them into the large crowd, swaying left and right. "I repeat," the captain announced, "if you persist you will be taken down."

The burly man hopped on one foot and the rest of the crowd started to waver. In truth, had they pressed on, they had the numbers to overwhelm the authorities, but many would die in the process. No one wanted to die, The Wraith could tell. He could see it in their eyes. Even so, he kept his body ready, his muscles tensed, in case he needed to take action once again. He hoped he wouldn't have to. In truth, he wasn't sure what more he could do. He looked over to Lady Wraith, who appeared just as tense as he.

A rather butch-looking lady stepped forth. "To hell with it, to hell with you all," she said. She rubbed at the back of her head. "I don't want to die today."

The crowd murmured likewise in unison. There had already been too many deaths, too much tragedy. There was only so much a person could take. This crowd had reached their limit.

"It's over," the captain shouted. "Return to your homes. Rescue authorities will be along as soon as they are able with further assistance and information. Please be patient."

There were further murmurings of discontent but the fight was now out of them. There was no going forward. A few more grumbles and they started shuffling back in the direction they had come. The Wraith looked to Lady Wraith again. He could tell she was frazzled but she held her resolve firmly. He moved over to her.

"It's over," he repeated the captain's words.

Lady Wraith smiled weakly in reply.

"I've let headquarters know backup's no longer needed here," the captain called out. He listened into his radio. The Wraith couldn't make out the words. The captain nodded and smiled broadly. "I'm hearing reports that all the riots have been quelled peaceably. We ultimately had the numbers in place to deal with the situation."

The Wraith placed his hands on Lady Wraith's shoulders. It was, indeed, over.

"What happens next?" she said, clearly exhausted.

"We start over," The Wraith said. "We rebuild this city, and we rebuild the trust with its people. Hope must be restored." He took a deep breath, turned to watch the crowd slowly disappearing down the street. "Hope for the future."

~ Chapter 12 ~

THREE WEEKS LATER

It was early evening and a deep darkness was already looming, with lengthy shadows being cast in all directions by Metro's high-rise skyline. Soon, the city would resemble a giant birthday cake, twinkling away throughout the otherwise murky night.

The Wraith was perched atop the Blooms Department Store building in downtown Metro, looking to the street below. Opposite was what had been, until recently, an abandoned store, formerly a Toys-R-Us before the chain went bankrupt. Now it had been taken over by the government and quickly refurbished into a mass vaccination center, similar to such centers that sprang up during the Covid-19 crisis a few years past. Despite the hour ticking past seven, there remained a long line of people waiting to enter, and a steady stream of those leaving, their lives saved.

But at what cost. The Wraith shook his head and closed his eyes. There still hadn't been an official death toll released, but he knew it must run into the thousands, perhaps many thousands. He dreaded to think it could be even higher than that but the possibility was certainly there. So much tragedy, so much pain. It was sometimes too much to take, but then he returned his gaze to the street below. The survivors there, and many more at similar centers scattered throughout the city, were hope.

The city's hope for the future.

It would be for them to rebuild and start afresh. Work through the pain and anguish. Create a better city, a better tomorrow. Because there was always hope. The Wraith felt it building within himself.

"Hey," a voice rang out behind him.

"Sloan," The Wraith said without moving an inch, his attention from the street never wavering. "Thank you for meeting here."

"Sure," Sloan said. "But why here?"

"This is where a new city is birthed," The Wraith said, indicating the building opposite. "This is where hope is reborn." He finally turned to face his friend.

"The CDC got things going in record time," Sloan said, lifting his cap and running a hand through his receding hairline. "Many lives were saved, *are* being saved." He peered over the building's edge. "Only we lost so many, too."

"But we saved many more. Always remember that. Hope."

Sloan shrugged, then a few moments later nodded in agreement. A few moments of silence passed between them then, finally, Sloan spoke up. "This city owes you a tremendous thank you. Without you, I'm not sure a vaccine would ever have been found. The city honestly faced obliteration."

"No thanks are ever necessary," The Wraith said, returning his attention to the vaccination center.

After some more silence, Sloan turned to leave. He took a few steps then stopped. "Did you ever find out who exactly was responsible for this...pandemic. Surely not naturally occurring."

"Definitely not," The Wraith said, turning back round to face Sloan. "I have no proof, but I know who was responsible. And I intend letting them know that I know."

Sloan raised an eyebrow. "And what of this big threat you warned me about? Someone coming?"

"I'm looking into it."

The Wraith said nothing more and again reverted his view back to the street below. The Wraith heard Sloan starting to move away.

"Sloan," he said. "Always remember...hope."

Sloan nodded slightly, The Wraith saw from the corner of his eye, then turned and entered the building's service elevator, leaving The Wraith alone to brood.

Latham, he thought. *I'm coming for you.*

* * * * * *

As was his wont of late, Latham was burning the midnight oil, seated at his desk in his office, which had become more of a home in recent times than his actual domicile. In truth, there wasn't much reason to be home, except for sleep, and that was ever harder to come by these days. Work was now all there was and, in a way, he was glad. With himself back at the helm, his city–his kingdom–was on the mend. He allowed himself a smile and a deep breath.

His reverie was destroyed when the window behind him exploded in a sea of shattering glass and aluminum siding. A gasp, and a large shape appeared crouched on the desk before him. It had been a long time since he had been greeted in such a manner, but he remembered it well. The disruption infuriated him.

"Oh, it's you," he said, keeping a lid on his emotions. "The door *was* open."

The Wraith reached out, grabbed Latham by the collar and yanked him up out of his chair.

"You're responsible for the deaths of thousands," The Wraith said through gritted teeth, spittle spattering on Latham's face. "You will face justice...and judgment." The Eyes of Judgment burst into life.

"Oh please," Latham said. "Your little guilt trip doesn't work on me, remember? I'm immune to your childish tricks."

The Wraith threw Latham back into his chair, causing Latham to grunt in pain.

"Whatever it takes, however long it takes...I *will* bring you to justice," The Wraith promised. He appeared enraged.

Latham smiled broadly. He knew it would annoy his great enemy. "Promises, promises. I assure you, I will remain at liberty. You have no proof of anything." He reached forward for his ornate ivory cigar case, opened it and produced a fine specimen of Cuban cigar from within. He lit it with a similarly ornate ivory table lighter, took a drag, and blew smoke rings toward The Wraith. "This city needs me. I'm leading the revitalization effort. Metro City will rise again. I will see to it personally."

"You're responsible for its near destruction."

Latham merely shook his head.

"Your company is nearly bankrupt. You're not capable of such massive expenditure," The Wraith said.

"Oh, haven't you heard," Latham said with a glint of pleasure, "my predecessor, the late, lamented Patrich Azufi..."

"Late?" The Wraith interjected, clearly caught off guard.

"Yes, my dear friend and former assistant. He wasn't the best at running my company in my absence, that is true, but he did get one thing right. He invested in a new tech start up. It was slow going at first, flew under the radar, but its new social media app, DayLight, has just gone...'viral,' I believe the word is. It's the next big thing, I'm told. It's reaping me millions. Likely billions. Who knows where it might lead." He was gloating now and enjoying doing so.

"Azufi," The Wraith said, getting angrier by the second from the look of it.

"Poor fellow," Latham said, a smirk never leaving his face. "He was found dead in the Gladstone area a few days ago. Died of grievous injuries, alone in some back alley. His body wasn't discovered for weeks the authorities tell me. Such a pity." He wasn't even trying to put on a mask of grief. What did he care of Azufi, of what The Wraith thought. His position restored, his kingdom soon reborn...nothing else mattered.

"Murderer," The Wraith grunted.

"Now, now," Latham said. "That's slander. Perhaps my attorneys need to have a word with you."

The Wraith grimaced. He must have known he was beaten. Again.

"You know the way out," Latham said, indicating to the open window. "Don't let me keep you."

The Wraith gnashed his teeth, appeared as if he may continue the argument, then no doubt thought better of such a futile exercise and leaped for the window ledge.

"You will not escape justice forever, Latham. One day you will fall. And I will be there to serve judgment upon you."

"Perhaps," Latham said, swiveling in his chair to face his enemy, "but not today. Goodbye."

The Wraith jumped out into the night, disappearing from view in an instant.

Latham sighed and brushed some glass shards from his shirt.

Bloody vigilante. I should send him the bill.

He smiled at that. Despite his serious injuries, despite all that he'd been through in recent times, he allowed himself the pleasure of feeling some measure of accomplishment. Yes, his original plans had come to naught, but even with a small hiccup along the way, he had still managed to come out on top. How ironic that that fool Azufi had done one thing right, and that investment had assured Latham's financial security. His victory. He had come up smelling like roses. Again.

He stood with some difficulty, and moved over to the sideboard and poured himself a glass of the finest Rémy Martin. He took a long, baleful sip, allowing the liquid to build in his mouth before swallowing. It burned his throat on the way down in a manner Latham found most pleasing. A thought suddenly came to him. He smiled and raised his glass.

"To you, Patrich, a toast," he said in jest. "The unluckiest son of a bitch known to man. But you saved me, restored my kingdom to me. I thank you."

He took another longer sip, swallowed, then laughed.

~ Epilogue ~

SIX WEEKS LATER

The Daimler pulled into the Sanderson House drive, the automatic gate closing behind it with a slight creak. Max piloted the vehicle through the home's expansive property, the driveway lined with Poplar trees, beautifully yellowing in the late afternoon fall sun. If one didn't know where the home was located, one could have sworn it was an estate in the country. Manicured lawns lay on either side of the drive, and garden beds featuring a variety of shrubs and flowering plants. Emily fairly gasped at her surrounds.

"It's all so pretty," she said, looking all around her. "And this...this is where I will live?"

"This is your home," Paul said, seated alongside the little girl in the backseat, Leena on the girl's other side. "Always remember that."

Finally, the car came to a stop under the home's front portico. Simpson was there to greet them as they exited the car.

"Welcome home, miss," Simpson said with a smile.

Emily took a little step back toward the car. She was clearly a little nervous. It was a lot take in, Paul realized.

"It's okay, sweetie," Leena said softly. "That's our butler, Simpson."

The butler took a little bow.

"What's a butt-ler?" the little girl asked.

"He helps around the house," Paul said. "I don't know how we'd get along without him. And..." Paul bent down to match Emily's height "...he's a master chef."

"Can he cook pasghetti?" she said with a giggle.

"The finest in town," Simpson said proudly as he escorted them all into the house.

"Thank you, Max, that will be all," Paul said, about to cross the threshold.

Max stared blankly at him, as though in a trance, then simply walked away, out toward the estate's ample garage. Paul wondered briefly at the odd behavior, but thought nothing of it, and entered the house with his family.

Once inside the lobby of the expansive home, Emily couldn't help but let out a low whistle. She was clearly impressed. Her previous home with her late-mother had been anything but fancy.

"I can't believe this is my home," she said under her breath, a shyness once again coming to the fore. "Thank you so much for taking care of me." Tears began welling in her little eyes.

Both Paul and Leena crouched down, Paul taking the little girl in his arms, her gorgeous long blonde hair cascading over his broad right shoulder. "We will always take care of you, sweetie. We hope you will feel at home here...with us."

"Thank you," she cried. "Thank you."

She yawned. It had been a long, drawn-out day. Perhaps early to bed was called for, Paul thought.

"You look tired," Leena said. "Would you like to see your room upstairs? Perhaps go to bed early?"

Paul smiled. Two minds.

Emily nodded. Paul picked the little girl up. She hugged him vigorously, then laid her head down on his ample shoulder. He heart melted. It was then he was sure they had made the right decision in adopting this sweet darling, if there had been any doubt. He carried her upstairs, with Leena in tow, and Simpson making up the rear.

Rounding a corner, down a lengthy hallway, then into a beautifully appointed bedroom, filled with the finest toys and books and decorated with a variety of popular cartoon characters. The name Emily Roseanne was emblazoned on the headboard of a sumptuous bed. It truly was magical.

"Do you like it?" Paul asked.

"I don't think she can hear you," Leena said softly. "She's asleep."

It was true: Emily had drifted off to sleep nuzzling Paul. He moved over to the bed and laid the little girl carefully down, making sure to tuck her into the goose-down doona. Nice and cosy. She turned onto her side almost at once.

"Thank you, Daddy," she whispered in her sleep.

Those words brought tears to Paul's eyes. Tears of absolute joy for the most part, but also because he knew this poor little thing had been through so much trauma recently. He could only hope the two of them could provide the stability and love Emily wanted and needed. He was confident they could.

He put a finger to his lips and the two tip-toed out and closed the door quietly behind them.

"She's such a doll," Leena said. "So sweet."

"She's been through Hell and back," Paul said. "I hope she can heal here and learn to love and trust again."

"She will, darling. She will."

Simpson hovered nearby. "Will Miss Emily be requiring dinner, sir?"

"I'm not sure, Simpson," he replied. "I doubt it, but remain on standby for a while in case she wakes up early."

"I will make a little something that can be easily re-heated later, perhaps."

"Good idea," Leena said.

The butler retreated down the hallway of the Sanderson House mansion. Paul and Leena slowly followed suit.

"Instant parenthood is such a big change to our lives," Leena said. "I hope we're ready."

"We're as ready as we'll ever be," Paul said as they reached the grand staircase leading downstairs. "Can anyone ever truly be ready for such a monumental occurrence in their lives?"

Leena seemed to agree with that sentiment.

"Love will win out, as it always does. As it always must," Paul said.

Simpson greeted them at the foot of the stairs, a look of grave concern etched into his hardened features.

"Simpson, what's wrong?" Leena said.

"Master Max," the butler said, "he sounds...not well."

"Max? Ill?" Paul said. He knew full well Max had never been sick a day in his life. He had the fortitude of an ox. "He seemed fine earlier. Where is he?"

"In the Lair, sir," Simpson said. "He said he needs your help immediately."

It sounded serious. Paul looked at Leena, who immediately nodded in return. Without another thought, they both headed toward the library. Paul reached the desk first, opened a drawer, and removed a small remote-control device. Pressing the button caused a small section of the adjacent bookcase to slide open with a whooshing of gears. An instant later, they were inside, descending in the small, oval elevator. Max stood sentinel-like beside the Lair's computer terminal. The back of the chair faced Paul and Leena.

"Max, is everything okay?" Paul said, noticing his friend was as rigid and emotionless as a statue. He was pale and unresponsive.

"You look terrible," Leena added. "You better come upstairs and get some rest. Maybe..."

"My master has been waiting for you," Max finally said in monotone fashion.

"Master?" Leena said. "What on Earth are you talking about?"

"He is referring to me," a deep voice emanated throughout the Lair.

It was a voice Paul was familiar with. He hadn't heard it for years, but it was something he could never forget. For the first time in years, he was truly frightened.

The chair beside Max pivoted to reveal the Cobra, alive and well as they had feared. His milky right eye shone and his smile revealed a cruelty rarely seen in any human being.

"I have returned," the Cobra said with menace. "Welcome me home."

~ Author's Note ~

I'm really quite proud of how this book turned out. Some might see it as filler material prior to the slam-bang *City of Fear* (the next novel in the series, which ties up the entire series' plotpoints to this point), but I think it became something much more than that. I hope you agree with me on this point.

Crime lord Robert Latham has always been the villainous focal point of the series. Other villains come and go, but he's always there, either in the forefront, or plotting away at the sidelines. He's always there. So, after what happened to him in a previous novel, *Vendetta*, I wanted to fully bring him back to the front of the action. Many of the stories feature fantastic plots and villains, but sometimes it's nice to just have a straight up crime drama—or something close to it—to help balance the series as a whole. I certainly hoped you enjoyed reading it. It's really for you, my loyal readers, that I do all this. Your continued loyalty and patronage means so much to me. I very much appreciate it.

As always, there's a sneak peek the aforementioned next in the series, *City of Fear*, and a look at the covers of the other books in the series. There will be more, many more, coming in the months and years ahead.

I'd like to thank my family, for always sticking by me, and all my colleagues and fans. You all play such a large role in everything I do. So thank you, one and all.

Until next time.
Frank Dirscherl
Wollongong, 2025

CITY OF FEAR

~ Sneak peek ~

Here is a special sneak peek at the following novel in the series, *City of Fear*. Please enjoy chapter 1 of this exciting book...

~ Prologue ~

The airship sped onward, up through the clouds, causing Natalya Blackova to rely on her instruments to navigate the craft. It was a cloudy night, with storms forecast to barrel down upon Metro city on the morrow. Magnus Khan sat in the chair beside Blackova, while the Cobra stared out the window.

Just then, The Wraith burst into the cockpit. Khan was the first to meet him.

"Time for round two," The Wraith said.

Khan growled as he began the battle, and while The Wraith's strength had been diluted, his anger, his determination, was stronger than ever before. Where Khan had been close to his physical equal in their previous encounter, his anger now knew no bounds. Evading each of Khan's blows, The Wraith lashed out, ending the battle with one powerful strike.

Blackova dared not react, for the craft had just experienced some slight turbulence and needed her full attention. Her master was on his own.

"Abdelkrim!" The Wraith boomed. "You will not escape me again. I have not forgotten your atrocities in Africa."

The Cobra growled with fury, and they battled there, in the cramped zeppelin cockpit, not only for their lives but the lives of everyone in Metro City. The struggle was fierce, with neither quarry gaining any advantage. Blows of inconceivable force were blocked and traded. There wasn't much room to evade them, and both combatants were soon showing the evidence of their battle. The Cobra finally lashed out with a strong uppercut, which slammed The Wraith into the wall opposite. Blood was splattered on the faces of both warriors, as they paused briefly, eyeing each other off.

"It is fitting to finish this here, above your beloved city," the Cobra said slowly. "We are the only two worthy to hold her in his hands." Then, as if in afterthought, he added, "After our previous encounters, and what you did to me, it is indeed fitting to fight for her here in the stratosphere."

The Wraith wiped the blood from his nose and stepped forward. "You let others fight your battles and flee like the coward you are. I did nothing to you. You *are* nothing! Metro City will never be yours."

"Then let us finish this now."

The Cobra launched himself at The Wraith, whose speed now failed him, and slammed into him, sending them both careening into the far wall. The Wraith grunted in pain as the Cobra reached for his throat, attempting to squeeze the life from him.

"You gave me this power I have," the Cobra snarled. "It was my destiny to receive everything from the old man."

The Wraith reached up, trying to break free from the villain's iron grip. "You were not worthy then...you are still not worthy."

The Cobra, furious, pulled him forward, never lessening his grip on his throat. He slammed The Wraith back into the wall repeatedly until he was close to unconsciousness. The Cobra did so for a fourth time, but this time the wall failed to hold under the incredible force smashing into it.

The Wraith and the Cobra plummeted out into the cold night, falling to their potential doom.

As they plunged through the icy air, The Wraith knew there was no hope of using his cloak to float to safety, not at this velocity. The only hope of survival was if he reached out for the ladder before it was too late. He had to move–*now*! Using his left arm–the stronger of the two since injuring his right in the leap for the rope ladder earlier–he grabbed the last rung and screamed in pain as his shoulder dislocated from its socket. Somehow, his fingers held tight and firm. Seconds later, the Cobra whizzed down past him and, in one last desperate grab for survival, latched on to The Wraith's ankle. He screamed and couldn't hang on with the added burden of someone the size and weight of the Cobra for long. Before his hand gave way, he thrust his right hand up and gripped the rung. His left arm now dangled lifelessly by his side. He knew, even with his good arm, he couldn't hold for long under the load of two large, heavily muscled men.

The Wraith looked down and saw his adversary staring up at him. The Cobra peered up with mocking eyes, struggling to maintain his grip on his enemy's ankle. The Cobra then grinned, as if he knew fate had somehow dealt him a different hand.

"Did I not say it was fitting," the Cobra shouted above the noise of the wind and the airship's engine, "to end this here? Indeed, although it is not the end I anticipated."

As his words were drowned out by the stark winds, his grip on The Wraith's ankle faltered...

...and he fell.

He didn't scream.

The Wraith, his body battered and bruised, pulled himself up and gripped the ladder rung under his right elbow. At least he was safe...for the time being.

Suddenly, the airship began to swerve, as if trying to shake him off. The Wraith realized that one or both of the two in the cockpit knew the Cobra was lost and was trying to gain retribution by shaking him off. He held tight with his remaining strength, but it was tough with the swaying of the aircraft and the now high wind threatening to loosen him from his perch. As impossible as the situation seemed with his injuries, he had to make his way back up to the cockpit. Slowly but surely, as the airship buffeted in the storm, The Wraith struggled to the top. Finally, he staggered inside the cockpit, and saw Khan still lying prone on the floor.

Natalya Blackova remained at the helm of the airship, now rocking wildly, due both to the impact of the storm and to her mad attempts at revenge against The Wraith. The Wraith's mind reeled–what was he to do? He had to take control of the ship, but he knew it wouldn't be easy, and he barely had the strength to stand, let alone engage in another battle. Did she even know he had returned to the cockpit? Perhaps he could surprise her and end this with little effort.

Before he had a chance to conceive a plan of action, Blackova whirled and fired a high-powered pistol at him. "Die!"

The Wraith managed to evade the initial barrage, but the bullets kept coming, and one found its mark in his upper right thigh, shattering his femur. The Wraith shouted in anguish, retreated, slipping back through the large opening caused by his previous battle with the Cobra. He gained a firm hold at the top of the ladder. Gaining control of the ship and landing it safely was no longer an option, not in his physical condition, and staying aboard the cockpit was clearly impossible. As it was, he could hardly consider what course of action to take next; his pain was indescribable.

No sooner had he lamented the current situation, the zeppelin banked downward sharply. He could barely hang on. The airship careened down through the clouds and the burrough of Gladstone's skyline quickly became visible.

The Wraith was helpless as Blackova madly banked the ship, aiming for the nearest tall building. His mind raced.

Is she so insane with rage as to sacrifice her life in order to get her revenge on me?

The Wraith dangled there, his left shoulder badly torn from its socket, his right shoulder strained to the limit, blood flowing from wounds to the face and thigh. He tried to gather his thoughts. It couldn't end this way. To have defeated the greatest evil he had ever known, only for his own end to come so soon after victory.

No, not now.

With the ship dangerously close to the building, it banked upward sharply, sending the rope ladder toward the building at great speed. The Wraith knew there was only one hope and a slim one perhaps. Sliding down the ladder as far he could, he prepared himself. Seeing a window close by, he let go of the ladder and crashed through it, and a desk behind it, before smashing into the wall at the far end of the empty office.

He lay there, finally able to rest. He'd survived. Somehow. Unconsciousness beckoned, and in the seconds he had remaining he knew it had been worth it despite what he'd been through. The Cobra had been defeated and a great pall had been lifted from the city. To save his city, to rescue innocents, he would sacrifice all, even his life, in his endless war against evil. This day, he had survived, barely, and while some had escaped, the Cobra had perished in battle.

As these thoughts drifted through his mind, blackness enveloped him.

* * * * * *

LATER THAT NIGHT

Metro City truly came alive at night. By day, it was a bustling metropolis like so many others. Business people flocked here and there, from office to coffee shop and back, meeting place to meeting place. Shoppers scurried about the main streets, using the high fashion boutiques as a playground. But it was nighttime when the shadows slithered forth, engulfing all that was good in the city in its inky, wicked embrace, and giving the city its dreadful reputation. Evil latched on to the city and its people as soon as the sun set, and it was loath to loosen that grip come the following morning.

Down by the dilapidated Christopher Docks in the now largely disused historic waterfront district (long since replaced by more modern facilities further along the coast), a dense fog billowed and rolled in from the Atlantic. Horns blared, the sound of waves slapped against the wharf pylons and a few small ships moored there bobbed up and down in the darkness as a large human form emerged from the water with a burst of froth and bubbles.

The lumbering form clambered up onto the rickety wooden structure, his weight causing the dock to moan and creak in abject protest. Collecting himself, heaving the air back into his lungs, he slowly trudged through the haze, marching silently out toward the abandoned warehouses.

Entering a dark alley, he rounded a corner and entered another, one of an infinite number located in that part of the city. The figure passed a series of homeless people and hookers plying their filthy trade in the nooks and crannies of this area referred to as Hell on Earth.

As the hulking figure continued his lonesome journey, a drunk stumbled from a seedy bar and practically slammed into him. The drunk rubbed his eyes in a vain attempt to see more clearly.

"Aye, ye a big lad, ain't ye?" the drunk slurred.

The figure remained silent and continued his slow march down the alley. He passed the short, portly drunken man, unshaven and dressed in clothing that had seen better days, ignoring him completely.

"Aye!" the drunk said sharply. "Are ye deaf? I'm talking with ye, man."

The figure continued to disregard the drunk who struggled to catch up and finally grabbed his cape in an attempt to whirl him around. The drunk fell to the ground in the attempt.

"Ufff...ye bast..." he grunted as he labored to his feet.

The drunk stopped in his tracks, as the figure now focused his attention fully on him. Coming into the light of a nearby street lamp, the figure's facial features became apparent. A large, cobra-shaped scar–or tattoo–surrounded his right eye, which was a horrendous milky white. Shoulder-length jet-black hair surrounded a powerful, cruel face. He was wearing a red and black outfit, form-fitting and armored with metallic, golden serpents completing the look.

"Fool!" the figure boomed. "Do you not know who I am? Do you not know that I am to be master of this city?"

The terrified drunk struggled in a vain attempt to backtrack and flee. In doing so, he crashed against some nearby trash cans, and fell in a sloppy heap into the putrid puddle.

"The Wraith took much from me," the figure continued. "But his end will come. My destiny has been foretold. Nothing will stop me. Nothing will stop–"

The figure reached down and yanked the hapless drunk into the air with one powerful arm. He pulled the drunk in close.

"–the Cobra!"

The Cobra's right eye began to glow and crackle with an ethereal energy.

The drunk screamed.

* * * * * *

THE PRESENT

Paul Sanderson and Leena Patterson closed Emily's bedroom door softly behind them.

"She's such a doll," Leena said. "So sweet."

"She's been through Hell and back," Paul said. "I hope she can heal here and learn to love and trust again."

"She will, darling. She will."

Jonathan Simpson, the household butler, hovered nearby. "Will Miss Emily be requiring dinner, sir?"

"I'm not sure, Simpson," he replied. "I doubt it, but remain on standby for a while, in case she wakes up early."

"I will make a little something that can be easily re-heated later, perhaps."

"Good idea," Leena said.

The butler retreated down the hallway of the Sanderson House mansion. Paul and Leena slowly followed suit.

"Instant parenthood is such a big change to our lives," Leena said. "I hope we're ready."

"We're as ready as we'll ever be," Paul said as they reached the grand staircase leading downstairs. "Can anyone ever truly be ready for such a monumental occurrence in their lives?"

Leena seemed to agree with that sentiment.

"Love will win out, as it always does. As it always must," Paul said.

Simpson greeted them at the foot of the stairs, a look of grave concern etched into his hardened features.

"Simpson, what's wrong?" Leena said.

"Master Max," the butler said, "he sounds...not well."

"Max? Ill?" Paul said. He knew full well Max had never been sick a day in his life. He had the fortitude of an ox. "He seemed fine earlier. Where is he?"

"In the Lair, sir," Simpson said. "He said he needs your help immediately."

It sounded serious. Paul looked at Leena, who immediately nodded in return. Without another thought, they both headed toward the library. Paul reached the desk first, opened a drawer, and removed a small remote control device. Pressing the button caused a small section of the adjacent bookcase to slide open with a whooshing of gears. An instant later, they were inside, descending in the small, oval elevator. Max stood sentinel-like beside the Lair's computer terminal. The back of the chair faced Paul and Leena.

"Max, is everything okay?" Paul said, noticing his friend was as rigid and emotionless as a statue. He was pale and unresponsive.

"You look terrible," Leena added. "You better come upstairs and get some rest. Maybe..."

"My master has been waiting for you," Max finally said in monotone fashion.

"Master?" Leena said. "What on Earth are you talking about?"

"He is referring to me," a deep voice emanated throughout the Lair.

It was a voice Paul was familiar with. He hadn't heard it for years, but it was something he could never forget. For the first time in years, he was truly frightened.

The chair beside Max pivoted to reveal the Cobra, alive and well as they had feared. His milky right eye shone and his smile revealed a cruelty rarely seen in any human being.

"I have returned," the Cobra said with some menace. "Welcome me home."

~ Also Available ~

The Wraith Dread Avenger of the Underworld #4
CULT OF THE DAMNED
Frank Dirscherl

With the city back firmly in his grasp, crime lord and entrepreneur Robert Latham is celebrating by bankrolling Metro City's 200th anniversary gala year, which includes the unveiling of a never-before-seen ancient Aztec stone carving—the Cortes Stone—at the City Gallery, a carving that has thrilled the scientific and artistic communities, but infuriated the monstrous Aztekoth.

NOW AVAILABLE!

www.glowingeyesmedia.com

The Wraith Dread Avenger of the Underworld #5
CRY OF THE WEREWOLF
Frank Dirscherl

Having gone through ordeal after ordeal, Paul Sanderson (aka The Wraith Dread Avenger of the Underworld ®) and his love Leena Patterson, decide to take a long overdue vacation. However, their idyll is soon shattered by an attack by a creature nobody thought could possibly exist—a werewolf. Soon, an evil so heinous makes himself known, and only The Wraith could possibly defeat it.

NOW AVAILABLE!

www.glowingeyesmedia.com

The Wraith Dread Avenger of the Underworld #6
SWAMP WITCH OF SATAN'S FOREST
Frank Dirscherl & Ray MacKay

On their way home from their mountain vacation which was anything but, Paul Sanderson (aka The Wraith) and his love Leena Patterson are waylaid by a mysterious cry for help, and are unwittingly drawn into the forest—and the web—of the alluring Swamp Witch.

NOW AVAILABLE!

The Wraith Dread Avenger of the Underworld #8
LADY WRAITH
Frank Dirscherl & Adam Oravec

The Wraith is missing. No one has seen him since going out on patrol. Now, the love of his life Leena Patterson, must sally forth on her own as Lady Wraith, protect the city, find her love, and combat a deadly new adversary hell-bent on destruction.

NOW AVAILABLE!

www.glowingeyesmedia.com

Books of Judgment Book Three
RISING SON
Frank Dirscherl & Adam Oravec

Robert Latham, Metro City's pre-eminent businessman and entrepreneur. He's also the head of the largest crime cartel on the east coast, the web in the center of the city's web of evil. But how did he become the all-powerful figure within the city. Growing up with nothing, he built his empire from the ground up, through strength, determination, and cold-blooded intimidation.

COMING SOON!

www.glowingeyesmedia.com

About the Type

Garamond is a group of many old-style serif typefaces, originally those designed by Parisian craftsman Claude Garamond and other 16th century French engravers, and now many modern revivals. Though his name was written as 'Garamont' in his lifetime, the typefaces are generally spelled 'Garamond'. **Garamond Normal**, used in this book, is one of those modern revivals.

Join FRANK DIRSCHERL and Glowing
Eyes Media on social media!

facebook.com/glowingeyesmedia

@glowingeyesmedia

instagram.com/glowingeyesmedia

@glowingeyesmedia.bsky.social

glowingeyesmedia.proboards.com

Want to be The Wraith?

Well, it might be hard to actually *be* The Wraith, unless of course you, too, have been endowed with the power of the Eyes of Judgment. But you can certainly dress, drink and drive like him [*] (and you don't always have to be a millionaire to do so). See for yourselves.

The Wraith/Paul Sanderson wears:

- tailored clothing from Cad & the Dandy Tailors and Shirtmakers – www.cadandthedandy.co.uk
- bespoke footwear from Gaziano & Girling – www.gazianogirling.com
- watches from Héron (Marinor in Atlantic Blue) , Erebus (Ascent 36mm in Enamel Black) and Jaeger-LeCoultre (Reverso Tribute Monoface Small Seconds in Opaline) -

   www.heronwatches.com/collections/marinor/products/marinor-atlantic-blue | www.erebuswatches.com/collections/ascent-36mm/products/ascent-36-black-enamel | www.jaeger-lecoultre.com/au-en/watches/reverso/reverso-tribute/reverso-tribute-small-seconds-q713842j
- Armani Code cologne from Giorgio Armani – www.giorgioarmanibeauty-usa.com/for-him-armani-code/for-him-armani-code,default,sc.html

drinks:

---

[*] Please note: Glowing Eyes Media does not condone drinking and driving. **All** adults, please always drink responsibly and **never** drink and drive

- Twinings Earl & Lady Grey tea – www.twinings.co.uk
- Vittoria coffee – www.vittoriacoffee.com/
- The Balvenie Scotch whisky – www.thebalvenie.com
- Armand de Brignac champagne – www.armanddebrignac.com
- Cosmopolitan cocktails

uses:

- Dell laptops – www.dell.com.au
- Chesterfield furniture from Abbey Furniture
  www.chesterfieldfurnituremelbourne.com.au
- wallets from Launer – www.launer.com
- a Samsung Galaxy J5 Pro cell phone –
  www.samsung.com/latin_en/smartphones/galaxy-j5-2017/SM-J530GZDITPA/

drives:

- a Rolls Royce Wraith – www.rolls-roycemotorcars.com/en-GB/wraith.html

And, if you're really eager to actually look like The Wraith—in full costume—then you can always head over to Xtreme Design FX and let Lance Coulter there make you an exact replica of the costume used for The Wraith motion picture – www.xtremedesignfx.com

HÉRON

GLOWINGEYESMEDIA

Héron Marinor in Atlantic Blue - The Watch For Superheroes

EREBUS

Erebus Ascent 36mm in enamel black

GLOWINGEYESMEDIA

www.ingramcontent.com/pod-product-compliance
Lightning Source LLC
Chambersburg PA
CBHW051120260626
47170CB00005B/1601